WREXHAM COUNTY
FOLK TALES

WREXHAM COUNTY
FOLK
TALES

FIONA COLLINS

The
History
Press

First published 2014
Reprinted 2019

The History Press
The Mill, Brimscombe Port
Stroud, Gloucestershire, GL5 2QG
www.thehistorypress.co.uk

British Library Cataloguing in Publication Data.
A catalogue record for this book is available from the British Library.

ISBN 978 0 7524 7689 6

Typesetting and origination by The History Press
Printed in Great Britain by TJ Books Ltd, Padstow, Cornwall

CONTENTS

ACKNOWLEDGEMENTS

Many people have given me help and inspiration while I have been writing this book. I should like to thank first of all my partner, Ed Fisher, for his beautiful illustrations; Katharine Soutar for the cover picture and Declan Flynn and Ruth Boyes, my editors at The History Press, for their patience and confidence.

My thanks to staff at Wrexham County Borough Library and Information Service; to staff at Wrexham County Borough Museum and Archives, especially Jonathan Gammond and Karen Harris; to staff at the A.N. Palmer Centre for Local Studies and Archives, especially Joy Thomas; to staff of Wrexham Countryside Services, especially Liz Carding and Martin Howarth; to members of the Wrexham Heritage Forum; to members of the Brymbo Heritage Group; to members of Brymbo Local History Group, especially Brian Gresty; to staff and pupils of St Mary's Aided Primary School, Brymbo, especially Rachel Roberts; to everyone who contributed memories to Wrexham Countryside Services' Pontcysyllte and Cefn Mawr Community Arts Reminiscence Project; to Siân Owen, who asked me to create a Welsh language story tour around Wrexham County Borough, and to the coach load of intrepid Welsh learners who came on the tour with us; to members of the Glyn Ceiriog branch of Merched y Wawr; to my friend and fellow Welsh learner David Mawdsley for advice on railway matters; to Anne Uruska and Iestyn Daniel for help in finding the poetry of Richard Gwyn; and to my friends and fellow storytellers Michael Dacre, Amy Douglas, Nicola Grove, June Peters, Mike Rust and Dez and Ali Quarrell for their help in finding, shaping (and sometimes pronouncing!) material.

The books and online resources that I have consulted are listed in the bibliography. They have been essential, and I have benefited greatly from the work done by those who have explored this material before me, including Alfred the Great's biographer, Asser; the Victorian adventurer George Borrow; and Wrexham's contemporary collector of ghost stories, Richard Holland.

However, it is to the people of Wrexham that I owe my greatest debt, for the stories, poetry and information they have shared with me in the old way, by word of mouth (and sometimes by its modern cousin, email). Most especially I am grateful to Pol Wong, martial artist and Welsh patriot; to Colin Davies and Brian Stapeley of Brymbo; to Deryn Poppitt of Chirk; and to four variously crowned, chaired and eloquent bilingual poets of Wrexham County Borough, who are carrying the flame of an age-old oral and literary tradition: Siôn Aled, Les Barker, Aled Lewis Evans and Peter Jones. This book is dedicated to these four poets, Y Pedwar Bardd.

Introduction

The Seven Wonders of Wales
Pistyll Rhaeadr and Wrexham steeple,
Snowdon's mountain without its people,
Overton yew trees, St Winefride's well,
Llangollen bridge and Gresford bells.

This little rhyme was written sometime in the late eighteenth or early nineteenth century, probably by an English visitor to North Wales.

Three of these seven wonders are in Wrexham County Borough in North East Wales, and in this book you will find stories from Wrexham, Overton and Gresford as well as many other parts of this interesting *bro*, the Welsh word for one's local district.

The County Borough is a relatively new entity, having been formed in 1996 by uniting parts of Denbighshire and Flintshire with Wrexham Borough. However, the movement of frontiers is nothing new in this borderland part of Wales, and the national boundary with England has been redrawn many times over the centuries. A good example is Offa's Dyke, the seventh-century creation of a Mercian king, which was probably built as a defensive barrier between Mercia and Wales but now runs right through the middle of Wrexham County Borough. A common description in Welsh for someone who has moved to England is 'one who has crossed Offa's Dyke'. However, in Wrexham County Borough one can live to the east of the dyke and still be in Cymru Gymraeg, Welsh-speaking Wales. According to the census of 2011,

12 per cent of the population of Wrexham County Borough consider themselves Welsh speakers, and nearly 21 per cent understand and use some Welsh.

Wrexham itself is the biggest town in North Wales and the seventh largest in the country. Since the beginning of this century, there have been three campaigns to gain city status for Wrexham, but each time it has lost out, most recently to the smaller and quainter new city of St Asaph in neighbouring Denbighshire. However, in 2009, members of Wrexham Council were delighted when UNESCO awarded the status of World Heritage Site, one of only three in Wales, to Pontcysyllte Aqueduct, together with 11 miles of the canal it carries across the Dee Valley, on the grounds that it is 'a masterpiece of human creative genius'.

The town of Wrexham, or Wrecsam, as it is spelt in Welsh, dates back to at least the eleventh century and has variously been spelt: Writtlesham, Wrechessan, Wrightesham, Wriffam and Gwrecsam. Local poet Siôn Aled told me a shaggy dog story about how it was named after a tavern run by a certain Sam and his wife (*gwraig* in Welsh), which was known as *Tŷ Wraig Sam* ('Sam's wife's house'). However, the Clwyd-Powys Archaeological Trust suggests the Old English personal name 'Wryhtel' was combined with 'hamm', meaning a water meadow, to give 'Wryhtel's river meadow'. This, perhaps on the low-lying ground between the Gwenfro and Clywedog rivers, might have been the original settlement. It must be said that neither Sam nor Wryhtel are Welsh names!

And here is the tension that pulls at the heart of this borderland town. Should it look for its history, or indeed for its future, east towards England or west towards Wales? Roman remains have been unearthed to the west of the town, while Offa put his dyke right though the middle of it, as did Wat, whose earthwork lies parallel to Offa's Dyke at several points in the borough.

By 1161 there was a Norman castle at de Wristlesham, which has been identified with a motte at Erddig. Holt Castle was built by John de Warenne shortly after 1282, on land granted to him by

Edward I, creating one of the Marcher Lordships intended by their new English overlords to keep the Welsh in check.

St Giles' church was built in 1220, and by Tudor times Wrexham was a prosperous market town. In the industrial era it became the 'smoky valley' of collieries, furnaces and clay works, which George Borrow saw as he walked over the border into Wales in 1854. In 1952 Llay Main Colliery was the deepest pit in Britain, and the Miners Welfare Institute there was one of the largest in the country.

Now exhausted land is being reclaimed for housing and industrial estates and Wrexham is re-inventing itself as a tourist destination. Its country parks, historic houses, areas of industrial heritage and places of natural beauty are all worth a visit. So too are its people, who are full of tales, poetry, songs and ready wit.

Wrexham County Borough was the birthplace of two of Wales' foremost Welsh language poets: John 'Ceiriog' Hughes and I.D. Hooson, as well as the influential novelist Islwyn Ffowc Elis. The English language Welsh poet R.S. Thomas was curate in the Wrexham borderlands in the early 1940s at Chirk, where he met and married the artist Mildred Eldridge, and at Tallarn Green, about four miles from Hanmer.

Llŷr Williams, the fine concert pianist, is from Wrexham County Borough and so too are the members of the Fron Choir, or Côr Meibion Froncysyllte, as they were known locally before they hit the big time. Miss World 1961, Rosemarie Frankland, was born in the Wrexham village of Rhosllannerchrugog, a Welsh-speaking enclave which has its own unique dialect words for 'snow', 'that' and 'there'.

Wrexham influence abroad is felt at Yale University in Connecticut, for one of its main founding benefactors, Elihu Yale, had family connections in this part of Wales, lived in Wrexham after retiring from the East India Company and is buried in the churchyard of St Giles' church.

But it is not the famous, but rather the unsung heroes and heroines of Wrexham County Borough whose stories make up the backbone of this book. Jack Mary Ann, Mrs Five O'Clock,

Robin Ruin, Queen Eadburh, Lady Blackbird … you will meet them all in these pages. I hope you will feel you know this corner of Wales a little better as a result.

This book contains just thirty of the many stories with which Wrexham and its surrounding area teem; among those I've included are my favourites, as well as stories so well-known that they could not be left out if the collection were to be in any way representative – and also stories that were quite new to me and so delightful they had to be in …

But some of the stories I wanted to retell simply eluded me.

If only I could have found a shred of evidence to support a tantalising rumour that Lady Primerose of Berse Drelincourt had taken Bonnie Prince Charlie as her lover! That she secretly financed the Jacobite cause, even that he turned up unexpectedly at one of her parties in London, although in exile … all this can be verified, but – unfortunately for me – there is no way now of knowing if their relationship went any further.

If only I could have persuaded myself that Ruabon is named, not after St Mabon, the son of Bleiddyd ap Meirion, but rather after Mabon ap Modron, the lost hero who is rescued from prison in the great ancient tale of 'Culhwch and Olwen' by two of Arthur's knights, riding up the Severn Bore on the back of the giant salmon, which is the oldest of all creatures. However, to connect the story with Wrexham was a leap of faith too far, so I contented myself with retelling but then discarding that tale.

There are many more Wrexham folk tales than I could include, so I apologise if a story you hoped to find here is missing. You will not read about Brymbo Man here or any of the Sir Watkins Williams-Wynns who declared themselves 'Princes *in* Wales' over the generations.

But I hope you *will* find stories to delight you, to make you squirm, or snigger, or snooze …

If you like these stories, please take them and tell them in your own way. They belong to us all and are worth passing on. There is an old kind of wisdom in the tales, which should not be lost in this careless modern world.

And if you don't like these stories, then please come to Wrexham County Borough to find some you do like. Come by train, bus, coach, car, canal boat, kayak, bicycle, motorbike or on foot, like George Borrow, to search out the stories that speak to you – and tell them instead! I shall look forward to hearing them.

Wrexham County
Location of the Tales

N

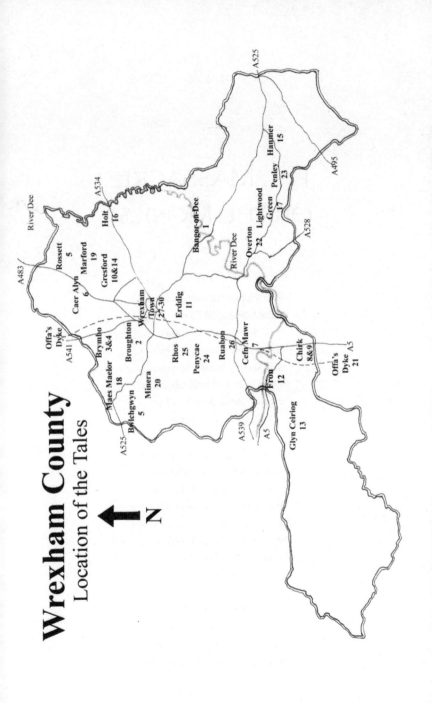

1

The Massacre of the Monks

When the heathen trumpet's clang
Round beleaguered Chester rang,
Veiled nun and friar gray
Marched from Bangor's fair Abbaye;
High their holy anthem sounds,
Cestria's vale the hymn rebounds,
Floating down the sylvan Dee.
O Miserere, Domine!

On the long procession goes,
Glory round their crosses glows,
And the Virgin-mother mild
In their peaceful banner smiled:
Who could think such saintly band
Doomed to feel unhallowed hand!
Such was the Divine decree,
O Miserere, Domine!

Bands that masses only sung,
Hands that censers only swung,
Met the northern bow and bill,
Heard the war-cry wild and shrill;

Woe to Brochmael's feeble hand,
Woe to Aelfrid's bloody brand,
Woe to Saxon cruelty,
O Miserere, Domine!

Weltering amid warriors slain,
Spurned by steeds with bloody mane,
Slaughtered down by heathen blade,
Bangor's peaceful monks are laid;
Word of parting rest unspoken,
Mass unsung and bread unbroken;
For their souls for charity,
Sing, O Miserere, Domine!

Bangor! O'er the murder wail!
Long thy ruins told the tale,
Shattered towers and broken arch
Long recalled the woeful march:
On thy shrine no tapers burn,
Never shall thy priests return;
The pilgrim sighs and sings for thee,
O Miserere, Domine!

Written by Sir Walter Scott and set to music by Ludwig van Beethoven, 1817.

The massacre described in this poem is part history, part legend. Certainly it is historical fact that a great monastery once stood on the bank of the River Dee, in what is now Wrexham County Borough. It was described as 'the mother of all learning' but was so completely destroyed that archaeologists have found no trace of a religious centre that housed over 2,000 monks and an unknown number of lay brothers. The poet, however, is unlikely to have been correct in his assumption that there were also nuns there, for there is no evidence that the monastery at Bangor-on-Dee was a 'double-house' of the type established at Much Wenlock, Shropshire, by St Milburga.

When trying to reconstruct events which took place so long ago, history and legend soon collide. According to the *Anglo-Saxon Chronicle* and *Brut y Brenhinoedd*, its British equivalent, the battle recalled in this poem took place in AD 604, though more recent scholars give the date as AD 616. The historical facts of this blood-bath are difficult to determine. Legend, however, is quite definite in its version of events.

It was St Dunod who established the monastery of Bangor-on-Dee, or Bangor-is-y-coed, as it is named in Welsh, in the late sixth century. In the ancient verses known as the Welsh Triads, it is named as one of the Three Perpetual Harmonies of the island of Britain, for 2,400 monks lived there, divided into groups of 100. Each group 'continued in prayer and service to God, ceaselessly and without rest' for an hour at a time each day, so that there was never a moment when words of worship could not be heard there.

When St Augustine arrived in Britain from Rome in AD 597, his mission from Pope Gregory was to convert the pagan Angles of the kingdom of Kent to Christianity. The king of Kent, Aethelberht (sometimes called Ethelbert), was married to Bertha, the Christian daughter of the King of the Franks, so it is possible that he was already a Christian before Augustine arrived.

Augustine, having won over and baptised many of the Saxons, turned his attention to the Christians in the west of Britain. He wanted them to acknowledge the supremacy of Rome and accept the Pope as head of the Church; this the British were loath to do, as their Church had a tradition of its own, reaching back to the Romano-British era. However, they were prepared to enter into dia-logue with Augustine, and so the seven foremost bishops of Wales agreed to meet with him at a certain tree, known as Augustine's Oak, on the borders of Herefordshire and Worcestershire. The bishops were accompanied by monks from Bangor-is-y-coed, as it was regarded as a great seat of learning.

On their way, the monks met an old man, who asked where they were going.

'We are going,' they said, 'to meet Augustine, who was sent by one he calls the Pope of Rome to preach to the Saxons. Now he asks us to obey him and to follow the ceremonies set out by the Church of Rome. Pray tell us, what is your opinion on this subject? Shall we obey him or not?'

The old man answered, 'If God has sent him, obey him.'

'But how can we know whether he is sent by God or not?' they asked.

'If Augustine is a meek and humble man, listen to him, but if not, have nothing to do with him.'

'How shall we know whether he is proud or humble?' asked the perplexed monks.

'That is easily done,' said their advisor. 'Make your way to the appointed place slowly, to make sure that Augustine arrives before you and takes his seat. Now, he is only one, and I know that there are many learned and respectable men among you. If Augustine receives you humbly, you will know it at once, for he will not remain seated while you stand. But if he does not rise from his chair to greet you, you will know that he is a proud man. If this is the case, do not obey him.'

The monks accepted this advice gratefully, feeling that the old man must have been sent by God to help them in their hour of need. They thanked him and made their farewells, continuing their journey at a steady but slow pace, to ensure that they arrived after Augustine, so that the simple test proposed by the old man could be put into action.

When they reached the oak, they saw Augustine seated under its canopy in an elaborately carved chair, with seven empty chairs arranged around him, ready for the bishops of Wales to join him. However, as the monks approached, Augustine made no move to stand or even to greet them.

Instead, his face cold, he launched straight into a speech: 'Dear brothers, though you hold many ideas contrary to our customs, yet we will bear with you, as long as you will, at this time, agree with us in three matters: to observe the feast of Easter according to the ways of the Church of Rome; to perform the ministry of baptism in the manner practised by the said Church; to assist us in preaching the gospel to the Saxons. If you will submit to us in these matters, we will bear with you, for a time, in other matters now in dispute between us.'

The monks exchanged glances. One of the bishops stepped forward to speak for them all.

'We will not follow the Church of Rome, nor will we acknowledge you as our Archbishop,' he said. 'For as you were too proud to rise from your seat to greet us today, how much more will you despise us if once we submit to your authority?'

The chronicler gleefully records that Augustine's blood 'boiled within him' as he replied.

'Is that your story? Perhaps you will repent later. If you do not think it proper to join us in preaching the gospel to the Saxons, the time will come, and come soon, when you will receive death at their hands!'

This concluded the fruitless meeting. The bishops and monks of Wales returned to their homes, shocked by Augustine's threatening words, but more convinced than ever that they had done the right thing in rejecting his proposals.

Augustine, however, set out to make sure his prophecy came true by urging the newly-converted Saxon king of Kent, Aethelberht, to take up arms against the troublesome Britons. Aethelberht raised his war band and called on his fellow Saxon, Aelfrith, king of Northumbria, to join him. The two armies set out for the flood-plain of the River Dee, where now it marks the border between Wales and England, Wrexham and Cheshire.

From the decaying Roman stronghold of Chester, Brochfael, grandson of the great Powys leader Brychan Brycheiniog, prepared to defend the land and its people. He sent heralds to the Saxon leaders to sue for peace, but the Saxons killed the messengers and sent back their bodies as a silent and deadly answer. The battle which followed is known in the Welsh Triads as the Contest of Bangor Orchard.

Out from the monastery came a solemn procession of hundreds of pious monks, who had fasted for three days and were not afraid to die. They came to support Brochfael with the power of prayer, and gathered at the side of his troops, singing and calling for divine aid with such loud and united voices that Aethelberht demanded to know who they were.

'We are the priests of the most high God,' rang out a voice from the throng, 'come to pray for the success of our countrymen against you!'

When he heard this, Aethelberht was furious, and ordered his men to attack the monks. The monks of Bangor-on-Dee put up no resistance, nor made any attempt to defend themselves but fell like barley at the harvest before the Saxon long knives, still singing as long as there was voice left in them. Then the Saxons turned on Brochfael's troops and continued the slaughter. Bede calculated that about 1,200 monks who had come there to pray were slain that day, and only fifty or less escaped in flight.

The battle was a decisive victory for the Saxons and of great strategic importance in their campaign to control the island of Britain, for it pushed a wedge between the British kingdoms of Strathclyde and what is now Wales, leaving both increasingly isolated.

The Saxons went on to raze the monastery to the ground: no trace of it remains.

2

JACK MARY ANN

Jack 'Mary Ann' Jones lived in Broughton at No.12 Top Boat Houses, Stables Road, Moss, with his long-suffering wife. She, of course, was Mary Ann.

They had a little stone house in a terrace on the hillside, with an excellent view down onto the single-track railway between Moss and Ffrwd. In fact, there was a good chance of seeing a train passing while you were sitting in the petty, the privy at the bottom of the garden, as long as you left the door ajar.

Jack worked for a while in the signal box on the GWR railway line down the valley. He might have worked there a lot longer if it hadn't been for an unexpected visit from the district signalling inspector.

'This is just a routine visit, Jack,' said the inspector, 'so I'm hoping you won't mind answering a few questions.'

'Fire away,' urged Jack cheerfully.

'Very well.' The inspector took this as permission to give Jack a true grilling. 'Say a passenger train were coming towards you up the line, but a coal train, heavily loaded, were running away downhill at speed because of a brake failure, and both were on the same track. As signalman, what would you do?'

'Well, now,' said Jack, looking confident, 'I'd pull these levers here, which would move the signals to Danger, and that would let the two drivers know they need to brake.'

'Very good, Jack, very good,' nodded the inspector approvingly, 'but suppose the signal wire were broken and the signal failed to operate?'

Jack Mary Ann

'Then I'd change the points, fast as a nail in a sure place, and set the road to switch one of the trains – probably the downhill – into the sidings.'

'Ah, but what if the points were jammed and couldn't be moved?' asked the relentless inspector.

'Well, there'd only be one thing left for me to do,' said Jack after due deliberation.

'And that would be?' prompted the inspector.

'I'd run like hell to the Clayton Arms for Dic Dal-Deryn. He's bound to be there. Then we'd both get back here as quick as …'

Jack got no further because the inspector interrupted him.

'Just hold it a minute! Why would you be fetching this Dic Dal-Deryn? He's not a railway employee, is he? What good would he be in this sort of trouble?'

'Well, no good at all, of course,' agreed Jack, 'but we're old mates, you see, and I know he's never seen a train crash either.'

Sadly, this encounter, and particularly Jack's attitude to the inevitable disaster the inspector had conjured, brought a sudden end to a promising career with the railway. However, never downhearted for long, Jack applied to join the police force instead. While waiting for his application to make its way through the official channels, he thought he'd have a night out with his friend Dic Dal-Deryn – a night poaching. Dic was an expert in this field, as shown by his nickname, which means 'bird catcher'.

Dic and Jack arranged, over a pint in the Clayton Arms of course, to meet late on the night of full moon.

'I'll call for you from your house about two, Jack,' said Dic. And so it was agreed.

Mary Ann went to bed at her usual time, but Jack said he would sit up a while longer before he followed her upstairs. Though she knew Jack well enough to be sure that something was up, Mary Ann simply sighed, kissed the top of his head and left him by the fire.

Jack was dozing in his chair when Dic tapped gently on the door. And tapped again. By the time Jack finally stirred, Dic was bashing at the door like one possessed. Upstairs, Mary Ann lay still, apparently fast asleep but actually listening to every word.

'Jack, come on, Jack *boi*. Open up! What are you waiting for?'

Dic's voice whistled through the keyhole, passed Jack's snoring form and made its way upstairs to reach Mary Ann's ears. She waited for Jack to respond, quietly amused to notice that he was almost as slow in replying to Dic as he would be to her.

'Hmm? Umm? O, yes, Dic, yes, I'm coming. I'll be right there.'

Blearily, Jack picked up his jacket and let himself out the back door. Mary Ann heard it close quietly behind him. She settled down with a sigh. Dic greeted Jack with another sigh.

'What took you so long, Jack? I've been here for ages … let's get going!'

'I just need to go to the petty first,' said Jack, 'I shan't be long.'

Dic almost groaned in frustration, but then thought: 'Fair's fair, when a fellow's got to go …'

He leaned on the wall, while Jack blundered down the path to the privy, his jacket over one shoulder. Dic gazed at the moon and waited. And waited. And waited. Five minutes went by. Ten minutes went by. Why was Jack taking so long? Dic's thoughts worked their way slowly from annoyed to concerned to worried. At last he decided he had better go to see what the matter was.

As he went down through the garden, Jack appeared from the privy at last.

'You've taken your time,' said Dic.

'My jacket fell down the hole,' said Jack. 'I've been all this time trying to fish it out with a stick.'

'*Duw*, boy, you won't be able to wear that again, even if Mary Ann were to wash it for you,' said Dic, wondering why on earth Jack had wasted valuable time on such a thankless task.

'Well, I know that,' replied Jack scornfully, 'It's not the jacket I'm bothered about. It's my butties – they're in the pocket!'

Up at the bedroom window, Mary Ann stifled a snort of laughter and climbed back into bed.

It was only a few days later that a letter arrived, inviting Jack to present himself for training as an officer of the law. He embarked on his new career with enthusiasm, and was soon a familiar figure faithfully patrolling his beat. It did not take him long to get to know every inch of it, particularly the many taverns and ale-houses, which needed visiting frequently to make sure that everything was in order. Of course, it would have been churlish to refuse any refreshment he might be offered by the landlords he visited, all of whom needed to keep on the right side of the law, and hence of Jack.

Jack liked his ale, so he continued to frequent the many drinking holes of Broughton, just as he had done before he had his 'official' reason for being there.

One night, as he propped up the bar in the Clayton Arms, his helmet on the counter beside him and his pint in his hand, an unfamiliar figure pushed open the door.

'Is PC Jones in here?' asked a deep unknown voice.

Jack saw the glint of metal buttons and heard the unmistakable heavy tread of standard-issue police boots.

'I am,' he said, coming forward into the light, pint glass in hand, 'and you must be the new Police Sergeant.'

There was no reply, as Jack's newly appointed senior officer stared in disbelief at the unkempt and unsteady figure of his constable.

Jack put his head to one side and admired the Sergeant's trim uniform, before breathing beerily into his face, raising his glass in a toast, and saying: 'You've got a good job there, *boi*, so mind you hold onto it as long as you can, for sure as eggs is eggs, I've just lost mine.'

In this, as in so many other things, Jack was quite right, and the long-suffering Mary Ann found herself once more trying to make ends meet and keep body and soul together, without a penny coming in from Jack.

Soon they fell behind with the rent. It didn't take long until they were so far behind that it seemed as though the landlord might have to pay them to live there. Instead, of course, he sent his agent with a notice to quit. Jack was home alone at the time and saw the agent coming towards the house. Recognising him for what he was by the hat on his head and the papers in his hand, Jack didn't answer the door. The agent knocked and knocked, and when no reply was forthcoming, crouched down to push the envelope under the door. Jack looked around, his mind working overtime, and grabbed the bellows from the fireside. Pumping them vigorously, he blew the notice to quit back out through the gap under the door. The agent tried again. Jack puffed it out again. And again.

Shaking his head in frustration, the landlord's agent went round to the back door to try there. But Jack was ready, bellows in hand, and made sure that the papers fluttered out before they were properly in. At last the agent gave up, stuffed the papers in his pocket and turned away, muttering as he did so: 'I'm not surprised Jack won't pay the rent on a draughty old place like that.'

Jack felt pretty smug about this and thought he'd solved the problem, at least for a while. But the landlord came up with a more permanent solution, which, to everyone's surprise, didn't please Jack at all!

When the landlord himself came round, Mary Ann was in and Jack was out, probably at the Clayton Arms, where his 'slate' was so long they were thinking of using the roof. Mary Ann opened the door to find the landlord grinning insincerely at her.

'Mary Ann,' he began, 'this house isn't bringing me in any money. Not a penny. In fact, it's costing me, what with fees for the agents and the bailiffs and the legal expenses, so I've decided to cut my losses. I'm giving you the place. I can't be doing with it. You can have it, and much good may you have from it.'

He turned and walked away, leaving Mary Ann open-mouthed on the doorstep. She couldn't wait for Jack to get home to share the good news. So she took off her apron, put on her bonnet, and went up to meet Jack. When he saw her coming he braced himself for trouble, but Mary Ann's happy voice made him lower his guard.

'Jack! Jack!' she called to him, 'Wonderful news! Just wait till I tell you.' She came puffing up to him with a big smile on her face.

'The landlord has given us the house. It belongs to us. Isn't that good? No more rent – ever!'

Jack, however, did not seem pleased at all. In fact, he looked horrified.

'What made you say "yes", Mary Ann? Now we shall have all sorts of trouble. We haven't paid rent for months, but now we shall have to pay the rates! You should never have agreed to it!'

Mary Ann looked at him in exasperation, took off her bonnet and hit him with it, and stalked off without another word.

Not long after this, Mary Ann was feeling poorly in the night, so she asked Jack to go for the doctor. Now this was before they had both signed the petition for street lights up at the Pendwll and Boathouse end of the parish, and, with it so fearfully dark at night, and also Stables Road being a bit of a rough area in those days, Jack was afraid to go out so late all alone.

'But Mary Ann, *fach*, I know you need the doctor, so don't fret. I'll carry one of the kitchen chairs with me as I go. That way, if anyone threatens me, I can tell him we're flitting to avoid the rent, and that there are another five big fellows behind me with the rest of the chairs and the kitchen table.'

Even though she was feeling pretty sick, Mary Ann still managed a smile at Jack's ingenuity.

You'll be glad to know that Mary Ann was a pretty tough nut – well, she had to be, to be married to Jack – and she soon recovered. But she still had plenty to put up with …

Most weeks Jack would walk down to the Beast Market in Wrexham to see the auction. Mary Ann was glad enough to have him out of the house for the morning so she could get on with her work. She had been right through the house from top to bottom, and was on her knees on the doorstep, donkey-stoning the flags at the front of the house, when she saw Jack coming up the hill. And he was not alone. Following behind, as he led, was a goat!

Mary Ann got up off her knees, so she could look Jack in the eye, and folded her arms, to give him a chance to speak before she hit him.

'What's this then?' she asked, her voice worryingly quiet.

'It's a nanny goat, Mary Ann, *fach*,' answered Jack blithely, with the tranquil oblivion to impending danger of a man who has enjoyed a few pints.

'And what would we want that for, then?' she continued, a dangerous edge creeping into her tone.

'To give us free milk, of course, *f'merch i*,' he replied triumphantly.

'We haven't anywhere to keep it,' said Mary Ann, increasingly tight-lipped.

'Not to worry, *cariad*. The nanny can sleep under our bed, can't she?'

'Under our bed? Under our *bed*! What about the smell?' she almost – but not quite – yelled at him.

'O, Mary Ann,' said Jack cheerfully, ' The nanny goat will just have to put up with it, won't she?'

What Mary Ann said next has not been recorded!

3

THE TWELVE APOSTLES

Brymbo Hall in all its splendour – with colonnaded windows, a half-timbered frontage and gable ends sporting flamboyant finials – was an impressive house. Its grounds included magnificent avenues of horse chestnut trees, tranquil artificial lakes, ornate fountains and a fabulous outlook over the Cheshire plains. It had 'one of the most beautiful and extensive views in the kingdom', according to an enthusiastic estate agent, writing in 1829.

Built for John Griffiths in 1624, Brymbo Hall and its lands passed down from Mary Griffiths through the women of the line until, in 1792, it was sold to 'Iron Mad' Wilkinson. He had no interest in the house or its beautiful grounds, its appeal to him was in what lay below the ground: the deposits. Soon the site was covered by the furnaces, machine shops, cooling pools, rolling mills and railways of Brymbo Steel Works, which 'Iron Mad' had first set up as Brymbo Iron Works.

Not far from the house stood the circle of trees known as the Twelve Apostles, twelve lime trees encircling a single beech. The beech grew beside a well which had never run dry, and this was believed to represent the water of life. In the folklore of plants, lime trees stand for justice and truth. Traditionally village meetings all over Britain would be held under lime trees, which were said to be able to unearth the truth. The beech was believed by the Celts to be the tree of learning, wisdom and the written word. Some say its name is the root word for 'book'. I do not know who planted the original Apostles, or what significance they held at the time. They may have been, as their name implies, a Christian symbol. But a tree by a well is often an older, pre-Christian sacred site, especially in Celtic places.

The prophecy about the Twelve Apostles, which Brian Stapeley first heard as a lad from his uncle, and Colin Davies from his *taid*, or grandfather, goes as follows: 'If ever the trees and well are destroyed, only ill luck will befall Brymbo.'

Sadly, by 1972 even the prophecy could not protect them from the relentless march of progress, and the thirteen trees were cut down and sent to the sawmill, to clear the way for open-cast mining on the site.

Sure enough, after the circle was cut down, the steel works went into decline, though it was to linger for another eighteen years, shedding jobs and livelihoods all the while, before it finally closed, with the loss of a final 1,125 jobs. Ill luck indeed for the village!

Colin, who was the fourth generation of his family to go into the steel works, and Brian, who was a Brymbo community councillor for twenty-nine years, are two of the leading lights of the Brymbo Heritage Group. Together with Keith Williams and Raymond (who wouldn't tell me his second name!), they have created a new chapter in the story: the Heritage Group decided to research the story of Brymbo's Twelve Apostles and bring good luck back to the village by replanting the circle.

Theirs was not the first attempt to do so: in 1978 twelve trees were planted near a footpath. But as they had been mistakenly set out in a square, not a circle, it is perhaps not surprising that soon they were vandalised and burnt. Later, another attempt was made in a different but obviously wrong spot: again, the trees failed to thrive.

Early in 2012, Brian, Colin, Keith and Raymond met in the old machine shop of the Steel Works, as they have done most Sunday mornings since the Heritage Group was formed. There they took the first step in their plan to replant the Twelve Apostles. They spread out a 1912 Ordnance Survey map of their square mile and fathomed out where the tree circle had been. Then they thought about the huge changes that the site has gone through in its long and varied history, and worked out what the result would be if they replanted the trees in

their original location. Half the circle would be in the gardens of new houses built on the site of Brymbo Hall, while the rest would be some metres above their original plot because all the waste from the works, which has been used to level the site, has raised it.

'Where can we put them?' they wondered, perplexed.

'What about Number Six Pool?'

And so it was agreed.

When production at the Steel Works was at its height, there must have been at least six murky, sludge-filled pools into which wastewater from the cooling process was run. Two of these pools lay at the west end of the works, on either side of Middle Road, a causeway between them. In 1996, as part of reclaiming the works, one was cleared and cleaned, and is now a pleasant angling pool. The other, Number Six, also known as Bottom Pool or Hot Pool, has been filled in with rubble, boulders and soil, all cleared in the creation of a football pitch for the young people of the village. It is now a small rounded mound, overlooked by the much higher slope of Offa's Dyke. As Middle Road is no longer in the middle of two pools, Brian and Colin invited the children of the village school to come up with a new name for it, and it is now called Waterside Way.

Once the site had been chosen, permission for its use was easily won from Brymbo Community Council.

'We told them it will be called the Jubilee Circle, and this went down a treat!'

All the arrangements for funding the project, ordering the trees, getting donations of fertiliser from the council, and help with labour from the Groundwork Trust went amazingly smoothly, as though everything was conspiring to bring back good luck to the village.

Colin takes up the tale, which now moves from practical considerations to the realms of the magical – at least, I think so!

> Keith Williams was enquiring about trees. Groundwork offered us saplings, but we wanted mature trees. Keith reckoned they needed to be nearly thirteen feet high. He found us thirteen lovely trees, twelve limes and one beech, and the total cost, bought and delivered to site, was £313. They arrived on the 13th day of the third month, and were planted in a ceremony which began at 1300 hours. The first newspaper article about our plans was published on the 13th of January.

The preparation of the site was in itself something of a ceremony. The Brymbo Heritage Group, under Keith's guidance, determined the placing of the trees by pacing out the site. Colin told me:

> Keith said we must think of the future and plant the trees far enough apart for them to grow. He settled on the size of the circle and stood where the central tree would go. I went round the circle at the end of a twenty-metre rope, paced it out and banged in a stake each time. We didn't have a tape measure. When I asked how come I was doing all the hard work while they all stood in the middle, they told me: 'It's definitely a job for the Chair, Colin.' Well, the circle was 144 paces round, so we put the trees twelve paces apart. The only problem was that the first time I measured it out I was wearing boots. The second time I had my Wellingtons on and the spacing for the last tree wasn't quite the same. Mind you, if Raymond had been doing it we would have only had two trees altogether, he's got such long legs!

The tree planting was a joyful occasion, attended by the Mayor and Mayoress of Wrexham and the head teacher of St Mary's School in Brymbo, together with three of the school children, who helped to plant the first tree. This was officially the first event held in Wrexham County to celebrate the Queen's Jubilee in 2012.

The planting was blessed with good weather, and the month of March 2012 continued warm and dry. So dry that Keith, Brian, Colin and Raymond began to fear for the trees as the ground conditions were so hard. They decided that they had better carry water to the circle. Using all sorts of containers, they spent the first day of April carrying nearly 100 gallons of water to the thirsty trees.

Colin described a full day's work which left them all 'knackered'.

'I was alright,' said Brian cheerfully. 'All I had to carry was the camera.'

Ironically, next day it started to rain, and that April went down as one of the wettest on record. By the end of the month, the ground was well saturated.

'The good Lord with infinite wisdom must have been observing our efforts that day', Colin wrote in his record. 'He must have decided, "Well, boys, if that's the best you can do, watch me!" ' It was a cosmic April Fool.

At the time of writing, the trees are in leaf and flourishing. They have been able to establish themselves without suffering any of the vandalism which thwarted earlier attempts to replant the Twelve Apostles.

The last word should go to Colin. 'This was done by the community for the community. We were thinking of the old legends, hoping the good luck would come back. Will some good fortune return to the village? Only time will tell!'

4

ALICE IN THE CIRCLE:
ST MARY'S SCHOOL GHOST

Alice was a pupil at St Mary's School in Brymbo in Victorian times. She caused a lot of trouble at school and was often put in detention, having to stay behind after school. She was in detention on the night she died.

She turned on the tap and forgot about it. There was a flood, and the wooden floor in the hall actually rose up. Somewhere, there is a picture showing how the wooden floor had lifted because of the water. Alice died that night. But she did not leave the school.

Now her ghost lives upstairs in the attic, in the storeroom. Children from the school are full of tales of contact with Alice. Holly told me how Ellie and Ebony got locked in the storeroom last year: 'The door shut on its own. It's like it was locked. Miss Prescott unlocked it and got them out.'

Children in the school believe that if you take seven steps up the flight of stairs leading to the storeroom and shout 'Alice', then the ghost will speak to you. Chloe told me that there is also a rhyme you can sing – if you're brave enough:

> Alice, Alice, if you're here,
> Put up your hands and give us a cheer,
> Come down now and reappear!

Then, you must toss a coin. If it comes up heads, Alice will come; if it comes up tails, it will be her friend, Adam. Adam's the good

one and Alice is the evil one. Adam, it seems, could be a ghost from the same time.

Sometimes, if you turn off the tap and go out, it comes back on again by itself, and you might just hear a groaning in the boys' cloakroom or the door creaking loudly. Ioan remembered going into the toilet upstairs when he was little. He said: 'You'd feel cold all over and your belly would feel weird!'

Perhaps a cold breeze will go past you, or you might feel someone pull your hair – but when you turn around, there's no one there! Sometimes when the children are lining up to go out they hear creaking and banging coming from the top floor of the school. When he was much younger, Jack remembered seeing someone outside Mrs Masters' class who looked all white, like a white shadow, but when he turned back there was no one there.

The best place to look for Alice is in the circle window by the nursery playground. There you can sometimes see a white figure sitting in the window reading a book, or a glowing figure looking in at you through the window.

Holly has often seen a pair of red eyes as she turned off the light in the girls' cloakroom. Ellie, however, said the best place to meet Alice is in the library upstairs. There she once saw a pair of red eyes, looking out at her through the air vent, and a finger pointing … but to what?

5

FAUNA AND FLORA

ANN ROBERTS, BWLCHGWYN

Ann Roberts' family came from the Clwyd Valley, where she liked to go walking whenever she could. Truth to tell, she loved to go out and about anywhere in the area, whenever John Roberts was not at work, whether Saturday afternoon or on a holiday day. Some were not happy to see her wandering on the mountainside on a Sunday evening instead of going to chapel like everyone else. To make things worse, she would take her children with her on these little strolls. The other children thought that it would have been lovely to go walking on the mountain with Ann Roberts.

She knew how every creature lived and where it found its food. Whenever there was a heron on the lake, she would spot it, and no one saw the first curlew or swallow before her. She could tell you where the wild duck were nesting, and when you could find eels beneath the dam at Lake Maes Maelor.

The fox hardly ever had a chance to steal the chickens because Ann Roberts would see him off before he troubled her feathered flock. She could spot a snake at the side of the path before it saw her and knew when there were trout in the river before anyone else. There wasn't another woman anywhere in the neighbourhood who could catch fish by hand the way the lads did it. Ann would dip her hand under the stone where a trout lay and ten to one she would pull it out! She was a child of the open air and a lover of nature in all its many guises, and she could see something new in a place where others saw nothing. She caught hares in the wintertime if they came too close to Tŷ Top, which is what they called their home, and it was all up for a poor rabbit once Ann got on its trail. She didn't interfere with the grouse unless she was quite sure no one would see her. The gentry were much too keen on shooting the grouse themselves. Ann knew when to hold back and when to strike. She was rarely wrong.

Ann Roberts could neither read nor write, but she bought the paper every week and would get someone to read it to her by the fire in the evening. She was very interested in the picture papers that were popular during the time of the Boer Wars, and she spent a long time looking at the pictures of lads who had been killed in battle. She was as familiar with place names like Modder River, Spion Kop and Mafeking as she was with Pant Lladron or Casgen Ditw, home of Meredith Jones, the son of Ehedydd Yale. She felt deeply for those who had lost sons and husbands in that distant war, whoever they were. Even Lord Roberts, who lost his son in the fighting, received her sympathy. Some people wondered whether she secretly believed that John, her husband, and Lord Roberts were two branches of the same family. Whether this was the case or not, she truly was the kindest woman to all sorts of people. Even the pedlar, whom everyone knew as 'the old man of Llanberis', had no curses from her, and all the children in the area were her friends, since she had a very comfortable way with them.

Ann Roberts had no style when it came to eating or clothing. She would visit her neighbours' homes in her flat cap and apron, always ready for a chat with anyone who had a story to tell.

She was the only person in the community who served potatoes in their skin. At the time, this wasn't considered the done thing in good homes. But this didn't bother the housewife of Tŷ Top in the slightest. Done this way, she said, potatoes were really tasty, as well as being easier to prepare. Anytime a lad went up to the house, he'd receive a warm welcome to join her in partaking of potatoes, and anything else that happened to be going. She always ate plain food: potatoes in buttermilk, oven-baked onions, porridge and, of course, bacon.

As a rule, she had plenty of interesting tit-bits of gossip to share too: things she had heard from John, her husband, about his work or news from the frequent visitors who came round to her house and she to theirs. Some people complained that she was spreading gossip, but she had no taste for running people down.

Anything like books or education was relatively unimportant, in her view. Cutting hay and planting potatoes were much more important. People need to eat, and need to work before they can eat.

After keeping away for some years, she and her husband started to go to chapel, and the children then went regularly. It was clear that she and her husband enjoyed chapel, but she didn't take to it in any way that could be called 'godly'. She loved life and nature, and no one ever criticised her for this. She knew nothing about how to make money and was never seen to do a stroke of work. She had a strong constitution, a love of nature and her neighbours, and a delight in the simple life. Once she was gone, the place seemed empty without her.

Mrs Five O'Clock, Rossett

Gun Street in Rossett used to be the main road from Rossett to Marford, with traffic passing over a shallow ford through the River Alyn, which, when it rises, can flood the back gardens of the houses in what is now a quiet cul-de-sac. Vehicles and pedestrians now cross the river dry-shod, across the Mill Bridge, leaving the residents of Gun Street in peace.

This picturesque lane took its name not from memories of some ancient battle but from a public house partway down the street, originally called The Gun, which later changed its name to The Pig and Whistle. Fortunately for the residents, the street did not follow suit! Now the old pub has been converted into two private houses.

A little further down the street is a row of lock-up garages, where originally a terrace of small houses stood. Mrs Five O'Clock, whose real name no one now remembers, lived in one of these. The row eventually got into such poor condition that when they were put up for auction no one wanted them, which is why the owner had them demolished.

Whether Mrs Five O'Clock had a family or an income the story does not say, but she had a truly entrepreneurial spirit, which would probably be admired today, though it was rather frowned upon at the time.

Mrs Five O'Clock would note whenever a funeral was taking place. This was easily done, as Gun Street flanks the parish church, Christ Church, Rossett. A little after five o'clock the same day, before night rain or early morning dew had time to spoil them, Mrs Five O'Clock would make her way to the fresh-turned earth marking the grave of the churchyard's newest resident and carefully remove the ribbons from the wreaths on the grave, reasoning to herself, 'Well he (or she) won't have no more use for 'em now.' These ribbons were traditionally made of genuine silk.

Mrs Five O'Clock took them home, smoothed them out and sold them. Did she use the proceeds to support her family? Or perhaps they were for alms to give to those even less fortunate than herself? No, apparently she wanted the money for spending in the local gin palace. I'm not sure where that was to be found, but her path from Gun Street to the churchyard can certainly still be followed to this day.

6

THE KING OF
THE GIANTS

In the time of once upon a time, the court of the giants was held near what is now the town of Wrexham. Some say that the Iron Age hill fort at Caer Alyn, on the bank of the River Alyn, was the actual site of this mythical gathering, while others believe that the giants gathered at the Bronze Age round barrow called the Fairy Mound, now in a residential part of the town, in the garden of a house on Fairy Road.

Wherever it was, it was a famous court from which the king of the giants one day sent out the summons to a tournament. Lords far and near received the call, which invited them to send six knights to compete. Each knight was required to come bearing a bag of gold as his entry fee. The canny giants had worked out that if they then awarded some of this gold to the victors, they would cleverly avoid the necessity of providing any prizes themselves and might even make a small profit!

News of the tournament was received everywhere with excitement, the flower of chivalry eagerly making ready for the fray. And nowhere was the flower of chivalry more blooming than at King Arthur's Court. Arthur! The Once and Future King, with his fair queen and noble retinue of knights, whose legendary stronghold Camelot – at least for the purposes of this tale – was situated at Wroxeter, or Caer Guricon, as it then was known.

Six of Arthur's finest knights set out northwards to the giants' court; each with the requisite gold packed in his saddlebags. As they followed the curve of the River Alyn, they saw the pennons and banners of rival champions fluttering ahead of them, and by the time they arrived at the court of the giants, the air was bright with the jingle of harness and the ringing of horses' hooves.

There was feasting, there was minstrelsy, there was storytelling and boasting and poetry and song, and, at the end of the night, there was comfortable lodging for each knight and good stabling for every horse.

The next morning, the lists were ready and the champions prepared for the jousts. Ladies offered scarves and silken ribbons as favours to the knights who pleased them, to make them their champions. It made no difference whether the lady were a giant or of regular size, her favour was received with equal gratitude and honour, and worn with pride, displayed on the helmet of the chosen one.

The tournament was long and glorious, and competition was fierce. But Arthur's knights carried the day. To the victors the fruits: bag upon bag of gold to carry triumphantly home.

That night there was another feast, and Arthur's knights sat in honour at the high table of the king of the giants, listening late into the night to praise songs composed to their glory by the giant king's giant chief bard.

After so much excitement and late-night carousing, it is small wonder that Arthur's knights did not make an early start to their journey home the next day. There were favours to be returned, farewell kisses to be stolen and bags of gold to be stuffed into saddle bags, in the hope that they would pass unnoticed by any highway robbers who took it upon themselves to challenge such a glorious band of knights.

At last, the knights set out on their return to Camelot. They were well pleased with their adventure, and eager to reach home and tell their tales of derring-do. But it was not so simple. The journey home took them through dangerous territory, and in spite of their resolve to be well past danger before dark, their tardy start meant that they were still traveling as night fell.

As the darkness thickened, the knights began to feel uneasy, looking back over their shoulders repeatedly and jumping nervously at every noise. They were not sure of their path through the marshy flat borderlands and, as it grew darker, a thin grey mist began to rise from the damp ground, swirling round the horses' legs and making it still harder for their anxious riders to discern a safe path.

The ground was boggy and gave way alarmingly beneath the horses' hooves. The knights dared not stop to orient themselves, for fear of sinking too deep to be able to move on.

'We should dismount and lead the horses, to lessen the weight they carry,' proposed their leader. 'The gold in our saddlebags is already heavy enough. We need to pass as lightly as we may over this quaking bog, and find solid ground again as soon as we can.'

The knights obeyed reluctantly, immediately feeling their mail-shod feet sink into the ooze, which seemed to suck at the horses' hooves no less eagerly now that the men were prey to it too.

'Keep moving, friends,' exhorted the leader, 'no one wants to be stuck here for the night now, do they?'

But this attempt to lighten the atmosphere only seemed to make more concrete their worst fears: surely anyone who became trapped in the bog would be there a lot longer than one night ... long enough for his armour to rust and his bones to bleach, long enough for his bereaved family to mourn ... and then forget ...

They tried to put these gloomy thoughts out of their minds and go forward confidently, but the truth was that they no longer knew whether forward was in fact backward, nor which way was homeward, which led back to the court of the giant king and which led who knew where. They were horribly lost, with the mist thickening around them and the worst of the night still ahead.

They stumbled on, cold, frightened and wet, leading their equally miserable horses through the endless swathes of boggy, reedy ground. Water swelled up to fill hoof and footprints as soon as each foot was freed of the deadly sucking kiss of the mud. They had no idea of where to go or what to do, knowing only that they

must keep moving or sink inexorably into the slime. They expected the worst; suddenly, it seemed that the worst was going to be very bad indeed!

Appearing without warning out of the mist, an enormous gaping mouth opened before them. It was ringed with pointed teeth, and from it came a mighty roar. The knights recoiled in horror and their terrified horses squealed and plunged, so that their hooves sank deep into the deadly grip of the bog.

Gradually they made out the creature: it was not a disembodied mouth, as at first it had seemed to be, in the drifting mist. It was a white lion, huge in size, which seemed to shine and shimmer in the darkness as though it exuded light from within. Its eyes were red, and so, they saw, were its ears.

Anyone familiar with the *tylwyth teg*, the 'fair folk', knows that white beasts with red eyes and ears are their creatures. The knights quailed, feeling sure that a fairy beast was even more to be feared than a wild animal. But the lion did not attack. Instead, it turned and walked away from them for a few paces, then swung its great shaggy head to look back at them over its shoulder with those burning red eyes.

'It … it wants us to follow it,' blurted one of the knights. 'Will it lead us to our doom?'

'Or out of this infernal place,' suggested another.

His companions turned to look at the speaker.

'Perhaps the giant king has sent his beast to help us,' he said. 'Does his shield not bear the likeness of a white lion?'

This was true, and the knights looked again at the beast standing in the gloom. It was swishing its tail impatiently from side to side, but still it waited for them to follow and made no threatening move.

'Very well,' decided their leader, 'let us trust ourselves to it. In truth, we have little choice. We are well and truly lost, and without help I fear we will never find our path home. This is the help that is offered to us. We shall accept it.'

He tightened the reins of his horse, which stood blowing miserably at his side, mud halfway up its fetlocks. It raised its head and tugged at its hooves as he whispered encouragingly to it, until, with a sucking sound, one hoof pulled free. Man and horse began to plod after the beast, which passed as lightly over the mud as if it were on firm ground.

The rest of the band did likewise, exchanging nervous glances. But they need not have worried. The white lion continued to move steadily ahead, pausing now and again to look back over its shoulder as if to check that they were all still following its lead. Past shadowed hollows and dark pools they went, mud and ooze below them and swirling tatters of mist all about. The cold breath of the marsh was chill on their backs, but they kept their faces turned always towards the shining pelt of the lion, as if to a beacon of hope which went before them.

At last they felt firm ground beneath their feet. The horses whickered gratefully, and a weight of fear seemed to drop from the men's shoulders. They looked around. Though the mist still coiled about them, it no longer seemed full of menace. They recognised landmarks now, for the first time in a long time, and saw that they were not so far from a familiar way-marked track, which led from the giants' court back to Camelot.

The lion took a few more steps and then turned towards them. Once more it opened its red maw and roared. But they no longer felt fear. Instead they raised a ragged cheer in thanks, to which the whinnies of the horses were added. Amidst all this clamour, the lion's voice rang out clearly, being by far the loudest. Then, suddenly, it was gone! The knights' voices died away too in surprise: the creature had vanished. Not even paw prints in the mud remained to show that it had ever been there.

'A magical creature, indeed,' said their leader thoughtfully, 'and a mark of the true power of the king of the giants, that he can command such a being to his will.'

'Aye, and he knows when travellers are in need of his aid, even those who are far from him,' added another man. 'Truly he is a great and powerful king ...'

The others nodded thoughtfully, then, at a signal, gathered up their reins to mount.

'When we reach Arthur's court, there will be praise songs of our exploits in the lists,' their leader reminded them. 'But we must tell the tale of this journey, which so nearly ended with us all lost forever. We must make sure that the king of the giants and his white lion are honoured and remembered in story.' And they spurred their eager horses towards Arthur's court, towards home.

7

WARTIME TALES

In 2004 I worked on a reminiscence project with my friend and
fellow storyteller Amy Douglas, collecting memories from people
who lived in the Wrexham villages of Acrefair, Garth, Newbridge,
Pentre, Trevor, Cefn Mawr and Froncysyllte, all of which surround
Thomas Telford's Aqueduct at Pontcysyllte.

Many of the people we talked to had vivid memories of the
Second World War and its effects in Wrexham County Borough.
With grateful thanks to all who gave interviews, here are some of
their wartime tales.

CEFN MAWR

We all had pigs, and my sister Helena had one called Stumpy that
used to lie there, still as anything. We used to tell her it was dead
and she would bawl her eyes out. Our brother Michael had one
called Spot. I remember him chasing it around the village with a
mop because it had this big patch on its spots and he was trying
to rub it off. He chased it all round Newbridge trying to get it off.

When it came to the first slaughter, Dad took it to Harrison's
Farm, which is now Tŷ Mawr Country Park. We all said: 'We can't
eat that, Dad, it's our pet! Can't eat those!' We wouldn't eat our
pig – no way!

So I remember Dad tried rabbits then. I remember my dog, Basher, an Alsatian, coming down, and he used to collect them up, the little bunnies, and bring them back to us: he was a very gentle dog. But we couldn't eat them: they were pets! We didn't like the geese, so we didn't mind if it was a goose that was necked. I used to neck chickens and we didn't mind them at all, because they were violent, they pecked you.

So we tried vegetables. I remember Dad planting all the vegetables and the boys picking them up and checking the roots to see if they were growing. Of course they all had to be replanted, and then before the crop was even ripe, we used to pick them and eat them. So there was nothing left when they were supposed to be ready. So that went by the wall.

There he was. Our Dad. No money, no tobacco, no fags. So he decided to grow tobacco. We used to think that was lovely: lovely plants. We didn't know it was tobacco at first, we just saw nice strong plants, nice little flowers. Then we had to pick all these leaves.

'What you picking those for, Dad?'

'What are you hanging them from the ceiling for?'

They were like bats hanging everywhere: drying out from the ceilings, under the beds, everywhere. And then we had to put them with apple core and with rum, or with a bit of sherry, experimenting on the flavour.

We used to ask: 'What are you doing this for?'

'Smells nice, Dad.'

Until he started to smoke it! And then it was: 'Dad, have you taken your boots off?'

'No it's Dad's tobacco!'

'You better run, it's Dad's revenge!'

That was the only successful thing he ever grew, I think. Everybody knew about his tobacco.

DRIVING AT MONSANTO

When the war started, I went down to Monsanto Chemical Works, and I was the only woman holding a licence at that time, so either

I would be sent away or I could take the job of driving. So I went to go on to the big scamels. It's a three-ton unit and you have three big trucks, one was with a big cover, the others were flat and they're articulated. I was working the three big trucks with two men there.

I was only six stone two then and there were no self-starters or anything on them, and you had limited petrol then. You started it with a handle. So when I started first there was a wager on that I wouldn't be able do it, and I was determined that I *would* do it!

But in the meantime, Johnny, he was from Llangollen, he took me on to learn. We had to lock every gate then, because of sabotage or anything, so you had to keep getting in and out with the gates. I wasn't used to the big wagons behind me and I was very short, so I more or less had to lean straight out.

We came to the laundry gates and I leant out, and the next thing was: we took the gates with us! Poor Johnny!

'Oh Margaret!' he said, 'We will never do this!'

But I did!

At the main gates, we had to keep blowing the horn for the gatemen to come out. I found that if one gate was open I could get the unit through. But I came up with a truck and forgot, didn't I, so I took that other side gate off as well! I wasn't flavour of the month at the time.

AIR RAIDS

When the war came, nobody had shelters here. In fact, the first time the siren went, the next morning everybody said, 'What was that about?' It was like a ship's siren, and nobody knew what it was for. They found out afterwards, of course, that it was the air raid siren.

We didn't realise the danger we were in, I suppose. Uncle Fred next door, he was in the First World War. It had gone a bit quiet one night, and he went outside. He heard something – I don't know whether it was a bomb, or an aircraft – and he went flat on the floor, on the yard, because he'd been in the First World War, so he had some idea.

Under the cinema steps

Nobody had air raid shelters in the early part of the war, so Mr John Owen Jones allowed my father and Uncle Fred to put forms under the cinema steps, and we used that as our air raid shelter in the very beginning. You'd got the steps behind you, and you went under, so you'd got the overhead cover, and we used to sit there, until the all clear went.

Under the table

My nain had a steel table, and if anything happened, she went under the table. During this period, the siren would go and the headmaster would send you home. You'd come out with your gas mask, and if you'd been sent home it's serious, and the siren would be wailing away. The siren at Monsanto, that's the one they used.

In the pantry

I can remember, I lived next door to my nain and taid, and the two front doors were joined and we used to go in there in the war. They used to put me and my cousin in the pantry, there was a big pantry underneath the stairs – I don't know why they thought we'd be safer in there!

Enemy planes

The first time we heard aircraft, in our innocence we thought they were ours, until my brother, who was at Dunkirk, came home on leave, and he heard them and he said, 'Oh no, those are Germans.' There was a certain throb to the engines – a different sound, I suppose.

MARCHWIEL

WAR WORK

In the war, I worked in the Royal Ordnance Factory at Marchwiel. We'd go to Wrexham on the train and then they'd transfer us to buses. And some were open-top buses, from London and places like that. We'd go to the factory, and it was quite a big place: it was three miles, through the factory.

The units were mostly underground, and you were searched, you weren't allowed to take any matches or cigarettes, tobacco or anything inside the factory. You would go into your department, change your clothes for special clothes that they had (white top and trousers), and you would have a pair of shoes, with rope soles; you would take these shoes with you, and when you got to the unit, you would have to change your shoes. You weren't allowed to walk on the floors with any grit on your feet, in case you caused a spark.

Before you went out from the dressing room, you would be searched again to make sure you hadn't got anything on you that was contraband.

We worked three shifts: days, when you had to be there by six o'clock, afternoons and nights. It was quite dangerous. We were packing cordite. We used to have a break, and it was pitch dark. We had to go to the canteen. Occasionally they would have chocolate in the canteen, and we were allowed one bar.

With the open-top buses, in the winter we all used to try to get inside, because we went through what they called Spring Lodge in Wrexham and the children would be standing on top of a wall and would aim snowballs at us.

ACREFAIR

THE HOME GUARD

One night my mother had been upstairs and she was coming down.

'There's some funny noise here,' she said. 'Hey, Dai, come and listen to this.'

So they went in the front room and they were there listening, and what was it? The Home Guard on manoeuvres! They were crawling on their stomachs down the footpath. They hadn't got any arms, guns or anything. But she could hear the orders being given – 'Stop!' and so on. It was just like *Dad's Army*!

The village Home Guards were just like *Dad's Army* – it was hilarious really. Their captain, Joe Jones, wasn't a soldier but a solicitor's clerk. He was a grand chap. They had a sergeant, Harold Gough, who was a real soldier from the First World War, so he knew what he was doing. They'd be down on the Recreation Ground in Fron with broomsticks and all funny things, and I remember when we were up this tree and we were pelting them with twigs. We had no respect.

TREVOR

Did you know that the aqueduct was guarded by the Home Guard? They guarded it with shovels and brushes. They hadn't got any guns. What were they going to do if an enemy attacked: sweep them off the bridge or what?

GARTH

FIRE ON GARTH MOUNTAIN

The planes used to come over here to Liverpool, and at one stage they had to drop their bombs on Garth. It set the gorse a-fire, and it burnt for quite a while. Some people said a farmer had shone a light, but we understood they jettisoned the bombs. I don't actually know the truth of what it was but it certainly set the mountain on fire.

They didn't bomb the mountain for very long. The first bomb was dropped and it set the gorse on fire.

They thought they'd got something there and they bombed it the following night and the following night, for three nights, I think. One of the chaps in Dad's choir, who worked in the office in Monsanto, was sent to guard Garth Mountain. He was petrified! He was there all by himself and what he was guarding nobody knew. He had to stay there all night on top of the mountain. Apparently he was grey by the morning, he was so terrified!

FRONCYSYLLTE

BOMBING RAIDS

When the war came, there were no lights at all – pitch black. Therefore, everything was exaggerated. When the moon came out, it was absolutely brilliant because there were no lights anywhere. In Wynnstay Park they had searchlights and anti-aircraft guns. If they found an aircraft, all the searchlights would move across the sky to shine on the trapped aircraft. It looked beautiful, but I never heard a gun fire. The sky was black, with waves of German bombers coming straight over here to Liverpool.

I think they were making mistakes: they were dropping bombs all over the place.

COLLECTING SOUVENIRS

I used to like to chase aircraft that had been shot down or come down for some reason to get souvenirs, especially the glass (everybody wanted the glass because you could make nice things out of the Perspex from the windscreen).

One came down in Rhosymedre; I was on my bike there quick, before the police. One came down in Pentre, another on the castle, Dinas Bran, but that was in such a mess it frightened me, so I came from there quick in case I saw something I didn't want to see.

One night we were standing in the village, opposite the pub, and around the corner from Llangollen came an air transporter. It stopped right in front of us, and on the back they had a German Heinkel bomber, and they went into the Brit for a pint. We were up on this Heinkel bomber with our knives, having a wonderful time, getting the souvenirs. If you could get the German cross, which was the aircraft identification, you were lucky. You could easily cut a plane: it wasn't metal, only canvas.

Barrage balloon

I was sitting here one day and I saw a barrage balloon, with the cable hanging from it, drifting quietly up the valley. It must have broken away, but it was coming down, so I got on my bike. It came down just above the golf club, and I was there first. I had great big pieces of it, and all the lads were cutting it; the next few days in Fron all the mothers had these lovely big bags, made from barrage balloon material, for shopping bags.

Peace at last

I don't remember much, but I remember when it finished. They gave all the children a party in the Stute. It's not there now, they've got a community hall in Fron, but right by the side of the canal house was what we called the Stute. They gave the children a party there at the end of the war. They took us all to stand by the draw-bridge and somebody brought a radio out and there was the end of the war speech from Churchill. All the children from Fron were there and there were evacuees as well.

8

THE RED HAND
OF CHIRK

Chirk Castle has been the home of the Myddelton family since Tudor times. The family is real enough, but who can say whether the events related in this tale actually happened? The story explains the family's coat of arms. It can be seen at the top of the white-painted iron gates of the castle, where the Myddelton shield, emblazoned with three wolf heads, is surmounted by one lone piece which is not painted white: a red hand. Why the red hand? There are many stories about its significance, but this is the one that I find the most striking.

A long time ago, a lord lived in the castle. He and his wife had two sons. They were twins, born at the same time, almost the same moment, as each other. Even their mother could no longer remember which of them was the first-born.

Wanting for nothing, they grew strong and healthy: from babies to little boys; from little boys to bigger boys; from boys to young men. They were equal in everything: running, riding, wrestling, throwing, hunting – there was not one jot of difference between them.

And time passed, as time does, until the boys' father grew old and frail. At last, he found himself lying on what he knew to be his deathbed. He called his sons to him and spoke:

I am dying, and only one of you can inherit the title. I cannot choose between you: you are both equally dear to me, and equally capable of managing the estate. I could never make such a choice. But the choice must be made. So I have decided to set you a challenge. The next lord of these lands will be the winner of a horse race. You must set out together, pitted against each other, and race around the bounds of the whole estate. Whoever is the first to set his hand against the castle gate will be my heir. This is my decision. Good luck to you both, my dear boys.

And with that he sighed, and closed his eyes for the last time. The two youths were stunned. They gazed first at their father's body, then looked at each other, before quickly turning away, as if ashamed to be seen spying out a rival's potential.

When the period of mourning was over, when the funeral had been held and all that was needed had been done, the day of decision approached: the race between the two brothers for the land, the castle, the title and the power. To the winner would go everything; to the loser, nothing.

They prepared as thoroughly as they could, bringing themselves and their horses to the peak of perfection. This new challenge, so unlike any friendly contest that had ever arisen between them before, began to drive a wedge between them: there was too much at stake for either to feel warmly towards his rival.

By the time the day of the race dawned, the brothers were no longer speaking to each other: avoiding one another as they moved about the castle, glowering across the table when forced to meet in the awkward formality of meals. They kept their preparations for the race secret, silently weighing up each other's strengths and weaknesses.

In separate stables they groomed and saddled their horses, tightened the girths, checked the horses' hooves. Mounting, they adjusted the stirrup leathers, leaned forward to murmur in their eager horses' ears. Unaware and out of sight of each other, their preparations mirrored each other almost exactly, so much alike were they.

They met outside the great tower of the castle, where their mother waited to signal the start of the race. She looked from one to the other, but neither returned her gaze; each was staring ahead, picturing the challenge to come. She sighed, knowing that whatever the outcome, it would be joyful for only one of her sons, disastrous for the other. But there was nothing to be done. She raised her handkerchief without a word. There was nothing to say. She looked at her sons, saw them eager to be away. They turned to her, together, and nodded curtly to show they were ready to begin. She let the handkerchief fall – and they were off!

Swift as shadows, moving straight to the gallop from a standing start, the two horses sped away, beginning their circuit of the castle grounds, the riders standing in the stirrups, leaning forward eagerly to urge on their mounts. There was no difference between them: as ever, they were equally matched.

The horses raced along. They were neck and neck – the riders glancing quickly to one side, to check their rival's position, before turning again to stare straight ahead between their horses' ears, trying to pick out the fastest route, to spot any uneven ground or variation of the path that might give them the slightest advantage.

Halfway now, and still they were equally matched, no advantage to either, as the horses pounded on. It seemed as though their lives, intertwined from the very beginning, could not be separated, even by such a test.

But then, little by little, one began to pull ahead. A gap opened between them … it widened.

The brother whose horse was losing ground saw that he could not keep up with his adversary. He cried out wordless noises of encouragement to his horse, and kicked fiercely at the poor creature; but to no avail. It became clear that he was going to lose the race.

Now the great iron gates, finishing point of the race, came into sight. The leader looked ahead, then back over his shoulder, a self-satisfied smile twisting his lips. This, more than anything else, drove the losing brother into a frenzy. He tried everything in his power to close the distance between them, but there was no longer any hope of doing so.

Closer and closer to the gates they galloped, the leader already tasting the heady wine of victory. But the losing brother was on fire now, and unwilling to give up the inheritance, whatever the price. Seeing his brother approaching the gate, two or even three horse lengths in front of his own tiring beast, he pulled the dagger from his belt, and severed his own left hand!

The reins between his teeth, blood welling from the stump, he threw the bloody hand with all his strength. The ghastly object flew through the air, spinning as it did so, and struck the gate with a horrid sound, before sliding down it, leaving a red smear behind. This unspeakable deed won the day. Indeed, the first hand to strike the gate belonged to the brother who had been behind in the race. But in the particulars of the challenge, he had won. And so he was declared the victor, even as those who applauded him shivered at the deed.

The losing brother, his stomach churning with a mixture of disgust and envy, turned his horse's head, and without a word to anyone, rode away. He never returned. The new Lord of Chirk Castle waited only while his maimed arm was tightly bound to staunch the blood, before accepting the congratulations of his new household.

One of the first things he did as lord of the manor was to order a new coat of arms for the family, a red hand prominently displayed at the top, to act as a permanent reminder to all who saw it, then as now, of his determination to win the title, whatever the cost.

9

IN THE BLACK PARK

The sound of the breeze and the song of the birds filled the air beneath the canopy of trees. Small creatures stirred in the undergrowth and larger animals dozed in the shade.

The parklands of Chirk Castle were picturesque and peaceful. It was a lovely place. Yet at its heart lurked a dark secret. A little bothy stood by a lane near one of the streams which ran down to the River Ceiriog. Here, alone and isolated, a creature of power worked her wiles.

She seemed an insignificant old woman, yet a terrible force was at her beck and call, for she was in tune with nature and able to turn its huge energy to her will.

The Marcher Lord of Chirk knew nothing of her: she was beneath his notice as he went about his affairs. But whispers and rumours about the witch and her powers ran wild among the cooks, maids, gardeners, grooms, game wardens and huntsmen of his household.

Some were full of fear, while others took no heed of her reputation. Young Mary Fuller was one of the former, and she always made the sign of the criss-cross to ward off evil whenever the witch was mentioned. Mary's sweetheart, however, was one of the latter and refused to accept that the old woman might wield any sort of power. Fortunately, this was the only point of disagreement between them, for Mary and Owen loved each other dearly.

Every evening, Owen would make his way across the parkland to the little estate cottage where Mary, a maid in the castle kitchen, lived with her parents. They would walk together under the trees, holding hands, laughing and exchanging shy kisses and planning out their lives together. Though Mary was very low in the hierarchy of the castle, Owen was one of his Lordship's most favoured huntsmen and knew that he could expect his master's blessing and bounty on a match that would ensure he did not leave the estate.

Every evening, after seeing Mary to her parents' door, Owen would make his way back to the mews, where he had his quarters. He always went through the deepest part of the forest, along the lane where the old woman lived. Mary would shudder and beg Owen to take the longer path home, to stay well away from the woman she feared. But Owen would laugh off her fears and stride away confidently into the gathering gloom.

Truth to tell, however, as he approached the old woman's place, he would always quicken his pace and turn away to avoid catching sight of her. His heart beat a little faster while he was near the old woman, as if her influence were making itself felt, whether he willed it or no. Much to his annoyance, only when he was safely past would he feel calm once more.

Owen never spoke to Mary of his uncertainty. He did not want her to think him lacking in courage, though in truth, she would have praised his common sense rather than called him a coward if he had sometimes chosen the path less-travelled. But Owen was stubborn and would not change his ways for fear of 'that old witch', as he dismissively called her.

Time rolled by, until one summer evening, as they strolled together, Owen asked Mary to marry him. She stood up on tiptoe to kiss him, and whispered a shy 'Yes' into his ear as she did so.

Both were delighted, as were family and friends, and preparations for a simple country wedding began, with early autumn the time of year in view. As the wedding day drew nearer, they would wander arm in arm through the parkland of an evening and often strayed much further than they meant, talking and dreaming of their future together.

One evening, they found they were walking along the lane that led past the old woman's hut, and as they drew level with it, they saw a shaft of light coming from the open door. In the light stood the old woman, caressing the muzzle of a huge antlered stag. The animal was licking the woman's face while she murmured to it in a language that neither Mary nor Owen could understand.

Owen was filled with anger to see one of the noblest animals in the park – and one for which he held a special responsibility – being fondled by the old woman he despised. He unslung his crossbow from his shoulder and brandished it threateningly at the old woman.

She seemed frightened by his fierce look and drew back into her doorway, though she shook her fist at him as she did so. The stag bounded away and vanished into the darkness.

Owen and Mary continued along the path, both silently dwelling on what had happened but neither wanting to speak about it to the other. They only began to feel more at ease when the lane joined the road. Then Mary began to talk once more about their wedding plans, and Owen smiled again.

However, in their hearts they felt that they had crossed a line. And they were not wrong.

The old woman planned vengeance for the insult. She was burnt up by anger that Owen should dare to threaten her and cared not a jot for the cost as she prepared a charm of deadly power, even though the risk to herself was equal to the injury she could inflict with it.

The witch brewed up a spell of transformation and used its power to take control of the body of the mighty stag. She left her own body, a lifeless husk, on the floor of her hut, and roamed the park as the antlered king of its beasts. The other animals avoided the spellbound creature, but they need not have feared. The stag witch had very particular prey in view and other magic to work.

It was Owen and Mary's wedding eve. They walked together, as was their custom, in the warm air of that early autumn evening, their arms around each other, talking happily about their plans for the future.

They were standing on the hill, looking at the silhouette of the castle against the night sky, when a sudden change came over the weather. The clear sky clouded over, the air chilled and a strong wind rattled the last leaves down from the branches. It began to rain, and within moments the soft patter of raindrops was replaced by the angry sound of a rushing downpour. Owen and Mary ran for home and shelter. Soon they were cold and soaked through.

As they neared Mary's home, which stood, so the story says, close to where Chirk Aqueduct now carries the canal across the valley, a horrible sight chilled their blood. A line of shadowy forms appeared, preceded by a ghostly light. Four headless figures led the procession, followed by a hearse moving as if of its own volition, with no horse or other creature to pull it. On the hearse lay a bloody figure, which seemed to the trembling Owen to have his own face. Mary must have thought so too, for she swooned in his arms. Behind the hearse came a train of weeping figures, among whom Owen recognised the pale faces of friends and family. He watched the flickering corpse light lead the procession towards the village church. There, among the great yew trees in the churchyard, it faded from his sight.

Mary hung heavy in his arms and his terror turned to concern for her. She was breathing in a shallow, gasping way. He lifted her up and carried her home. He knocked urgently on the door. Mary's mother opened it, to see her daughter pale and limp in the arms of her husband-to-be.

'Mother Fuller,' said Owen he gently laid Mary on the settle beside the fire. 'We have had a real fright. We have seen a corpse light, and Mary was greatly afeard. Can you settle her in bed, and persuade her it was a dream? I cannot bear to think that she will fret, when tomorrow is our wedding day.'

Mary's mother shook her head in horror as she bundled up her daughter in a warm blanket.

'Owen, what does it mean?' she asked.

'I don't know, Mother Fuller,' confessed the young man. 'I hope it is nothing, but it was terrible fearful …'

Mother and future son-in-law looked at each other for a moment over the motionless object of their love. They said no more, and Mary's mother busied herself to warm and comfort her daughter. Owen stood by helplessly for a while, then with murmured excuses, let himself out. He arrived home, chilled in body and soul.

He stripped himself and tried to rub some warmth into his limbs before falling, exhausted but wakeful, into his bed.

He tossed and turned for a great part of the night, but at last he forced himself to put the possible meaning of the vision out of his mind and think instead of his wedding day. Only then did he fall asleep.

Their wedding day dawned bright and clear, with a fresh breeze that blew away the remnants of the previous night's clouds, and with them, so Owen hoped, all traces of the dread vision that he and Mary had seen. When he saw her at the church in her pretty new gown, he determined to set aside his fears, and it seemed that the same was true for Mary, for as she smiled at him, her eyes lit up with joy.

Friends clustered around the newly married couple as they left the little church at Chirk, and cheered mightily as Owen kissed his shy new wife. Then they all set off for her house, where the wedding breakfast was waiting for them. As the party strolled through the parkland, Mary took it into her head to run on ahead, laughing and beckoning them to chase her. They followed, Owen in the lead, but Mary went into a grove of trees, weaving this way and that between their close-set trunks, so that soon she was almost lost from view. The group spread out, calling and hallooing in happy tones, until their merriment, and Mary's bubbling laughter, filled the air.

But suddenly another sound was heard: the crashing of some large animal through the undergrowth, accompanied by a harsh grunting noise. Then a huge stag burst out of the trees, its lowered head revealing the deadly tines of its many-branched antlers.

Owen knew it straight away for the animal he had seen at the witch's hut, and his blood ran cold.

'Mary! Mary! Run!' he yelled.

Hearing the fear in his voice, Mary came rushing out of the trees, looking this way and that. The stag saw her before she saw it and, turning, charged towards her. Mary screamed and fled in earnest. Though Owen and his friends, their joyful sport all turned to fear, tried to distract the animal, it followed Mary, and soon the distance between them was closing.

Owen's lungs were bursting, but fear for his beloved put wings on his heels. Soon he was near enough to fling his jacket, which he had torn off as he ran, over the head of the stag. It caught in the tines of the antlers and hung across the animal's face, effectively blinding it.

'Run, Mary! Run for home!' cried Owen, and Mary, her wedding dress torn and dirty, turned for home with a gulping sob, while Owen put himself between his love and the blundering beast.

The stag, enraged by the coat flapping in its face, bellowed and bucked until it shook off the jacket. Then it turned its renewed fury on Owen. He ran. It followed. Courageously he turned to face the stag, standing his ground as it charged him. As it approached, he sidestepped, caught hold of its antlers as it swung its head towards him and vaulted onto its back.

Owen's friends watched in fearful amazement as he clung to the antlers. The beast bucked and reared beneath him, frantically trying to unseat him. Owen held tight. With almost human cunning, the stag raced towards a nearby oak and crashed its flank against the trunk, breaking Owen's leg as it did so. He cried out but continued to hold on.

The creature reared again and again, then, having failed to rid itself of its unwanted rider, flung itself down and rolled on the ground. Owen, half crushed by its weight, was left sprawling on the ground as the stag lumbered to its feet, reared up and planted its front hooves on Owen's chest. It paused triumphantly for an instant, before it lowered its head and, bellowing wildly, gored him through the chest. Then the beast tossed its head, shaking his limp body from its bloodied antlers.

Its evil work done, it raced away into the forest, in spite of all attempts by Owen's friends to catch it. There was nothing for them to do but carry the dead body of the new-made, new-slain groom to Mary's home. There, his widowed bride crouched beside the untouched dishes of the wedding breakfast and wept over her beloved.

When she told the others what had happened the previous night, and of her conviction that the stag was the old woman's familiar, they set out in a mood of grim vengeance to the old woman's bothy. But all they found there was her dead body, cold on the floor. It seemed she had set her thirst for revenge above her own love of life.

Of the three of them, only poor broken Mary Fuller was left. She survived that day long enough to re-enact a chilling repeat of the vision she and Owen had seen on their wedding eve, as she walked behind his hearse to the little church. Attending the funeral were many of those whose spirits she had seen, though she had tried to deny it, in the phantom procession of that dreadful night.

Not many months passed before Mary, her spirit and heart broken by what she had endured, was laid beside Owen in the churchyard at Chirk.

The witch had had her revenge, and the parkland where the stag had killed Owen became known as the Black Park. For a long time, no one would go there after dark, though the bewitched stag was never seen again.

10

MINING TALES

In Pentre Fron Colliery, at Coedpoeth, the mine flooded suddenly on 27 September 1819 and eleven men were trapped underground. Two were rescued, six escaped and two drowned. The last man, John Evans, was given up for dead. After thirteen days it was at last safe to pump out the water. Searchers then went back underground to try to retrieve his body, and a coffin and shroud waited at the pithead, ready for the corpse when it was brought out.

However, when the search team reached the area where they expected to find the body, they were startled beyond belief to hear a voice calling to them. It was John Evans, who had survived against all the odds by eating his candles and licking water dripping from the walls!

John was brought out feeble but alive, and made a good recovery. The colliery owners marked his extraordinary survival by commissioning a portrait of John in oils from the painter A.R. Burt. His fellow miners, in a much more practical way, made a collection for him so that he would never need to go back underground.

John, so the tale goes, took his coffin home with him, and insisted on using it as a cupboard for the rest of his long life. He did not need it for its original purpose until he finally passed away, at the age of seventy-five, in 1865.

A much sadder ending marks the story of one of the worst mining tragedies in Britain. The Gresford disaster happened in the early hours of 22 September 1934, when 266 men and boys, including three members of the volunteer rescue teams, lost their lives in an underground explosion, when gas trapped in the long and inadequately ventilated tunnels caught fire. Only six men from the night shift in the Dennis section of the mine escaped the fire, and only eleven bodies were ever recovered.

The anonymous broadside ballad 'The Gresford Disaster' was reputedly penned by the one member of the Llay Number One Rescue Team to emerge alive from the pit. It sets out in stark words what happened and the bitter feelings of the miners over the shocking lapses in safety there.

> You've heard of the Gresford Disaster,
> Of the terrible price that was paid;
> Two hundred and sixty-three colliers were lost,
> And three men of the rescue brigade.
>
> It occurred in the month of September
> At three in the morning the pit
> Was racked by a violent explosion
> In the Dennis where gas lay so thick.
>
> Now the gas in the Dennis deep section
> Was packed there like snow in a drift,
> And many a man had to leave the coal-face
> Before he had worked out his shift.
>
> Now a fortnight before the explosion,
> To the shotfirer Tomlinson cried,
> 'If you fire that shot we'll be all blown to hell!'
> And no one can say that he lied.
>
> Now the fireman's reports they are missing
> The records of forty-two days;
> The collier manager had them destroyed
> To cover his criminal ways.

Down there in the dark they are lying.
They died for nine shillings a day;
They have worked out their shift and now they must lie
In the darkness until Judgement Day.

Now the Lord Mayor of London's collecting
To help out the children and wives;
The owners have sent some white lilies
To pay for the poor colliers' lives.

Farewell, all our dear wives and children
Farewell, all our comrades as well,
Don't send your sons down the dark dreary mine
They'll be doomed like the sinners in hell.

On the night following the explosion, the African-American singer and civil rights activist Paul Robeson was performing in the Pavilion in Caernarfon. When news of the disaster was brought to him, he announced from the stage that all the money from the concert would be donated to the Gresford Appeal.

A memorial to the dead was not erected until November 1982, when the old pit wheel was set up on Gresford Heath between slate pillars.

In the dangerous working conditions faced by miners every day, it is not surprising that superstition and folkloric beliefs flourished. Many miners believed that it foretold bad luck if they met a woman on their way to work. Others felt it was unlucky to pass a rag and bone merchant. Another thing that was sure to bring misfortune was to turn back on the way to work to collect something which had been forgotten. If a miner left his lunch in his *snapyn* tin behind, he would be more likely to rely on a friend sharing food with him than to return home for his own.

Good luck, on the other hand, came to any miner who was befriended by the knockers, or fairy miners. One such was Dic Humphries of Rhos, or Rhosllannerchrugog, to give its full name. He always worked alone and at night, and brought out huge

The Gresford Memorial

amounts of coal. Everyone agreed that he was able to cut such a prodigious amount of coal because he had fairy help at the coalface. His nickname was: *Y Safiwr Mawr* ('the great undercutter').

Ezekiel was another miner well known in Rhos. He had a dry sense of humour. One day he was walking along Cemetery Road when he had to stop for a coughing fit, the result of years of inhaling the coal dust. As Ezekiel stood there, leaning on the cemetery wall, coughing his heart out, the minister happened to come by.

'Bad cough you've got there, Ezekiel!' he said.

'So it is,' replied Ezekiel, gazing over the cemetery wall. 'But I know of one or two in there who would be very glad to have it!'

Many of the miners brought years of experience to the task, as the state of Ezekiel's lungs demonstrates. Others came brand-new to it, as this final story shows.

Dic Frondeg came up from the country to try for work in the pit. Until then, he had always been a farm worker, so he thought it best to try to conceal his ignorance of coal mining. Of course, he knew a lot about horses, and indeed his friends had advised him that the most likely way he would get work in the mine was with the pit ponies. So, when the manager interviewed him, he was able to give a fairly good account of himself on this topic. In order to try to impress the manager, he pretended to have already worked as a haulier in another pit.

'Indeed?' asked the doubting manager. 'Then tell me, what kind of lighting was in use in that pit, candles or safety lamp?'

'Well, I'm afraid I can't tell you,' said Dic, 'For I only worked on the day shift.'

It will come as no surprise to learn that Dic was not taken on for either the day or the night shift.

THE THREE~WAY CROSSROAD

It is Hecate, the Greek goddess often shown in triple form as maiden, mother and crone, who rules over crossing places like doorways, thresholds and crossroads. The three-way crossroad is especially associated with her, because of her triple form, and is a particularly magical place. It is said that Hecate, who has three heads, looks down each of the three paths and sees the past, the present and the future.

Oedipus was doomed by a prophecy to the terrible fate of killing his father and marrying his mother. He was separated from his family at birth, in a vain effort to avert the fate that had been prophesied for him. Then he met a man at just such a three-way crossroad. They argued, and eventually Oedipus killed the man, not knowing that this was his own father.

This, of course, didn't happen in Wrexham. But Wrexham has its own three-way crossroad tragedy, which was recorded for posterity in 1956 in the local paper, *The Wrexham Advertiser*, in an interview given by the last squire of Erddig, Philip Yorke III.

Philip Yorke went about town on a penny-farthing, played the musical saw, never threw anything away and lived without electricity in the damp and crumbling grandeur of his family's great house, using a portable generator to power his television set. He had been a traveling actor and a holiday tour manager before returning to

Erddig to become the squire in 1966, on the death of his older brother. The house was subsiding, due to the underground activities of the coal board, and eventually the upkeep of such a large estate became too much for him. Having never married and being without an heir, he handed Erddig over to the National Trust in 1973, on the condition that nothing was to be removed from the house. As a result, it is a treasure trove of domestic history, famous for the insights into life 'below stairs' provided by a series of portraits of the servants. The beautiful gardens are an important example of eighteenth-century formal garden design.

The story Squire Yorke told the local reporter concerns a man named Reynolds. Reynolds committed suicide in the 1790s, and was therefore, according to the custom of the time, denied burial in consecrated ground. Philip Yorke's eccentric style comes over well in the interview, and merits quoting verbatim.

Philip Yorke

My father told me that he knew a road-mender who had walked in the funeral procession of Reynolds, who had hanged himself in the wood somewhere up by Caesar Bank … I rather wonder whether this name may have had something to do with John Caesar, who was the trusted henchman of my great-great-grandfather Philip Yorke … the road-mender said that they carried Reynolds down the lane and buried him at the crossroads which is not a crossroads, and they drove a stake through his heart to prevent his ghost from walking. The object of the crossroads, I take it, was that should the stake fail to penetrate the heart, it was still a three in one chance against the ghost walking in your direction. But in the case of Reynolds it seems that the ghost would have no doubt as to which way to walk but back to Caesar Bank, the scene of his suicide.

Imagine the inconvenience of this for the good rector of Marchwiel as he returned after evensong past that point to his distant rectory ... it is, however, a well known fact that no ghost will pass a point in the road where a cross is clearly marked, so a cross was carved on the wall, and when we were children we used to get out of the pony cart and look for it, though I cannot remember now exactly where it was or what it looked like ...

What happened was that when the cricket field came into being at Marchwiel Hall, a part of the wall was reconstructed and another part of it was heightened, and the stone with the cross on it seems to have been turned round and the cross has disappeared inside the wall. Now, I have no evidence for stating this, but it seems to me that a cross is just as effective to a ghost when placed inside a wall as if it were clearly visible to the human eye on the outside. At any rate, I have not heard of Reynolds as having been seen beyond that point of recent years.

I do remember, though, my father telling me that there lived at one time at the Brook House, just below Reynolds' Grave, a man whose name was, shall we say, Arthur. When pubs in Wales were closed on a Sunday, he was in the habit of returning home by a different route from his usual one from The Waggoners at Gyfelia, and he never failed to give Reynolds a cheery 'Goodnight' as he passed his grave. But one night his 'Goodnight, Reynolds' was answered by a sepulchral 'Goodnight, Arthur' from deep down among the bushes. And Arthur ran headlong down the hill, which was steeper then than it is now, and over the bridge, which was more humpbacked then than it is now, and into the cottage like lightning, bolting and barring the door behind him. When he related his terrifying experience to his workmates, he was surprised to find that they treated the matter with more levity than he expected and suggested that the voice might have been that of one of his mates, who wanted to see whether he was capable of winning the hundred yards race in the oncoming sports.

A more recent and more probable appearance of Reynolds seems to have been in connection with a horse which my brother had before the war. This horse could not have been expected to know much about the events which took place there before he was born, coming as he did from halfway down the Vale of Clwyd, and yet, however tired he was on the way back from hunting, or at any other time, he always took the trouble to 'shy' whenever he passed that point after dark. My father was born 107 years ago [i.e. in 1849], and supposing the road-mender to have been something over seventy years old when they met, it would put the date of Reynolds' suicide as somewhere about the year 1790. And I rather hope that I may one day see a figure clad in the garb of the late eighteenth century seated upon that fine new concrete bench which a thoughtful council has erected there. And then if he can point out to me the exact position where the body lies, and if any remains are to be found, I daresay that by now quite a good case could be made out for having Reynolds re-interred in Marchwiel churchyard …

It is to be hoped that Reynolds' ghost took some comfort from the kindly intentions of the last Squire of Erddig.

12

THE RIVER THAT
RUNS IN THE SKY

The waters of the River Dee, yr Afon Dyfrdwy, run still and deep, turbulent and wild, as they flow from their source in the mountains of the west down to the sea. They have formed the landscape into a bowl, a fertile, sheltered valley where humans have lived since the earliest times. Humans have worked on this land and under the land too, digging out stone and clay and coal, using the gifts of the land and using the water too. It was Thomas Telford who drew the waters out of the Dee at Horseshoe Falls, channelled them into the Llangollen Canal for humans to use for commerce and industry, and carried them across the valley on the Pontcysyllte Aqueduct, that marvel of the Industrial Age, now a World Heritage Site. Pontcysyllte, pronounced '*Pont-kus-UCH-ti*', means 'the bridge that connects', and local people call the aqueduct 'the river that runs in the sky'.

The aqueduct carries the canal over the river on eighteen brick-built columns, which rise to a height of 121 feet. The water runs along a locally made cast-iron trough. The joints in the trough were sealed with red flannel dipped in boiling sugar, which Telford found to be most efficacious, and many of the original rivets are still sound and in place.

In the years since it opened in 1805, this amazing feat of engineering has attracted many famous visitors. They include

Queen Victoria, viewing this wonder of the Industrial Age, and Princess Anne, who flew over in a royal helicopter, much to the delight of members of the local Brownie Pack, who waved like mad. From the world of music, Felix Mendelssohn came to talk about tunes with the vicar of Rhosymedre, who was known locally as Big John Jesus. Much later, Harry Secombe was filmed for BBC TV singing the solo part of a hymn as he crossed the aqueduct by boat, accompanied by the Fron Choir down below on the playing field – where he could neither hear nor see them! As for stars of the big screen, when Harrison Ford and Calista Flockhart came on a narrowboat holiday in 2004, their overnight stay at the Bryn Howel Hotel was commemorated in the restaurant, where you can still order a Harrison Ford Burger.

One of the first visitors to record his impressions of the aqueduct was George Borrow, who set out in 1854 on the epic walk which is recorded in his travel book *Wild Wales*. He took lodgings in Llangollen for himself, his wife and step-daughter, and made a series of sallies around the locality from there, before setting out to walk to Anglesey and thence, eventually, round Wales to Chepstow. One of his earliest walks was a canalside stroll in the company of John Jones, a local shepherd.

Upon reaching the aqueduct, after a pleasant walk of about four miles along the towpath, the two of them stared dizzily down over the side at the river below and agreed that it gave them the *pendro* (giddiness) to do so. Borrow wrote down in his book exactly what John Jones told him: 'This is the Pontcysyllte, sir. It's the finest bridge in the world, and no wonder, if what the common people say be true, namely that every stone cost a golden sovereign.'

More recently, others have found its giddy heights tempting. In 2004, Patricia Diggory recalled a neighbour knocking on her door in the days when her children were still at school.

'Mrs Diggory, could you have a word with your boys when they come home?'

'Why, what are they up to?'

'I don't want to say any more, just have a word.'

Mrs Diggory was left with the awful feeling in the pit of her stomach which is familiar to parents everywhere. When the three boys came in, she knew only that they'd been 'about the wood and the aqueduct and so forth'.

'Where have you been?'

'O', they said innocently, 'We've been on the aqueduct.'

'Have you been throwing stones? What have you been doing?'

'Nothing.'

'Nothing? Well, Mrs Griffiths has been here and complained about the three of you. So I want to know just exactly what you were doing.'

'We were only walking along the aqueduct.'

'She wouldn't come here and complain if you were only walking along the path.'

'O, well, it wasn't *that* path, it was *that* one.'

They had been walking, not along the towpath, but balanced on the narrow outside of the trough, with nothing between them and the playing fields below but 121 feet of wild white air!

'I won't have you doing that again or you'll be in trouble,' said their mother, in a voice, considering the circumstances, of remarkable restraint.

Another example of derring-do by the young on the aqueduct comes from the 1920s, when there were still horse-drawn boats on the canal. Secondary school pupils living in the village of Froncysyllte had to cross the Dee valley on the canal towpath to catch the train to school. If they started on the narrow path over the aqueduct and a horse was coming towards them, they had a choice. Either they went back to where they had started, missed the train and were late for school, or they pushed through a gap in the railings and balanced on the outside, over the drop to the river, until the horse went past. Most chose the latter. It was, everyone agreed, mad what they would do to catch the train on time, and it sends a shiver down my spine to think of it!

Rumours of a ghost on the aqueduct provoke shivers of a different kind. Only one workman died during the long project overseen by Telford, which was a tremendously good safety record by the standards of the era. The man, whose name is not recorded, fell from scaffolding when the columns were being built. Some say that the ghost of that lone workman is still there, keeping an eye on the aqueduct and all who cross it.

Raymond Jones was convinced all his life that he had met the ghost when he was a young lad. He worked on the north side of the valley and lived in Froncysyllte on the south side. The shortcut across the 'akkie' was his regular path to and from work. One night he was returning home from a works outing to Blackpool, and was crossing the aqueduct in the dark. As he was walking along, he thought to himself: 'Now, a nice smoke on the akkie, looking at the stars, would be the perfect end to a perfect day.'

So he rolled himself a cigarette, but soon discovered, to his annoyance, that he hadn't got a light. He could see a man in the middle of the aqueduct towpath wearing dark clothes and a strange shaped hat, so he stopped and asked for a light.

The stranger didn't reply, just turned and proffered a lighted match for the cigarette. Raymond took a couple of paces past, then turned round to say 'Thanks, goodnight.'

But the man had disappeared.

There was no way he could have reached either end of the aqueduct in the time that had elapsed, and there had been no splash in the water, which was the only other place he could realistically have gone in the time. Raymond felt the hairs stand up on the back of his neck. Forgetting all about his cigarette, he turned and bolted for the end of the aqueduct, raced along the towpath to Fron Basin, ran up the hill to his house and dashed up the stairs to his bedroom. He jumped into bed, pulled the covers over his head and swore he would never cross the 'akkie' after dark again.

He always believed that he met 'a being of sorts' that night.

And who is to say he was wrong?

13

A LIVING WITNESS

The people of Glyn Ceiriog, the Ceiriog Valley, love to boast that the River Ceiriog is one of the swiftest-flowing rivers in Wales, tumbling down from the Berwyn Mountains and racing to join the River Dee. The valley it has carved, Glyn Ceiriog, was memorably described by David Lloyd George as 'a little bit of heaven on earth', and its steep upper slopes give way to lush pastoral land as the valley widens towards its mouth.

An exhilarating downhill dash over the fields from Chirk Castle and an athletic leap – or tired scramble – over a stile will bring you, breathless, to the valley floor at Castle Mill. Here, beside a bus stop, you can look across the B4500 and see an old stone bridge, which straddles both the River Ceiriog and the Welsh-English border. Just a little upstream, the swell of Offa's Dyke rises out of the southern side of the valley and marches away into England. In the flood plain between the river and the road lies a field of contented sheep. And to your left stands a truly ancient oak tree, a living witness of what happened in this sleepy spot more than 800 years ago: the Battle of Crogen.

This tree, more than ten metres in circumference, split in half during the fierce winter of 2010 after water inside its partly hollow trunk froze, expanded and burst it apart. The fallen side, still awaiting shoring-up, but supported by its lower limbs for now, has not come into leaf this year, though two healthy young birch trees grow from the humus in a cleft on one of the main, now nearly horizontal, branches. The standing side is burgeoning as I write, in late May, proving that this ancient tree, which has withstood so much, is still alive.

Deryn Poppitt of Chirk, who has made sure that the oak is now protected by a tree preservation order, has devoted years of time and energy both to this tree and to the remarkable story of the battle it witnessed: Crogen, a bloody skirmish between the warriors of Wales and the army of Henry II, ruler of the Angevin Empire, which stretched at one time from Scotland almost to the Pyrenees. Deryn took me to the river, the bridge, the dyke and the fields – the killing fields of the Battle of Crogen – all watched over by *Derwen Fawr Adwy'r Beddau*, which translates literally into English as the 'Great Oak of the Gate of the Graves'. Deryn, however, prefers its popular name, the Great Oak at the Gate of the Dead.

Deryn and his colleague Mark Williams were determined to change Crogen's status as a very small footnote in the turbulent history of Henry's reign, which is usually best remembered for Henry's military campaigns in Brittany, Toulouse and Ireland, his marriage to Eleanor of Aquitaine, the rivalry between his sons for their inheritance and the death of Thomas à Becket. Certainly, the tale of Henry's ill-fated campaign in Wales makes another great story from the annals of his times.

Henry II came to the throne of England in 1154, and his position, following the protracted struggle for power between his uncle King Stephen and his mother Queen Matilda, was insecure, to say the least. Born in Le Mans, he spent only eleven of the thirty-five years of his reign in England, and when there, he was usually busily engaged in trying to secure its borders.

In 1163 he thought the Council of Woodstock had solved the problem of his troublesome neighbours in Wales. But the fragile alliance lasted only two years before Henry's suspicions of Owain Gwynedd, ruler of most of North Wales, led him to go on the offensive. Mustering a huge army from his territories of Northern England, Brittany, Anjou and Normandy, as well as a large group of feared Flemish mercenaries, Henry marched to Oswestry on the Welsh-English border. There he set up camp.

Y Dderwen Fawr/The Great Oak

Meanwhile, Owain Gwynedd, aware of the danger brewing over the border, did what few Welsh leaders have managed before or since, and united a rare alliance of powerful rulers to face this mutual foe. Joined by Lord Rhys of Deheubarth in South Wales and Gruffydd Maelor, Prince of Northern Powys, he waited for the enemy force at the vantage point of the Iron Age hill fort Caer Drewyn, high up on the north side of the River Dee valley.

And nothing happened. As the summer of 1165 rolled by, the leaders of the two armies played a waiting game to see who would make the first move. It was Henry who lost patience and ordered his troops forward – but not into the Dee Valley, guarded from above by the Welsh forces on the hill. Instead, he followed the smaller river, the Ceiriog, into its valley, which lies south of the Dee Valley and runs almost parallel to it, with only a steep crest of the Berwyn Mountains between the two. Like much low-lying ground at the time, it was thickly wooded, almost impenetrably so.

But Henry was experienced and ruthless in dealing with such obstacles. Alongside his army of archers, spearmen and mounted knights, he had another: a force of woodcutters, some 2,000 strong. These he sent into the mouth of the Ceiriog Valley, with a party of archers and pikemen to guard them as they went about their work, and set them cutting a swathe through the trees to clear a path for the main body of his army.

This early example of the 'scorched earth' policy, a rapacious strategy still embraced by military commanders today, destroyed many fine trees. As Deryn Poppitt pointed out to me, from Castle Mill bridge down to the mouth of the Ceiriog Valley, no ancient trees remain. But upstream from that point is one of the oldest trees in Britain, the Pontfadog Oak, which was named as an official Great British Tree, to mark Elizabeth II's Golden Jubilee in 2002, when the oak was already at least 1,200 years old. And at Castle Mill itself, overlooking the place where Henry's axe-men were brought to an abrupt halt, stands the Great Oak, *y Dderwen Fawr*, saved from the English when a band of Welsh warriors ambushed Henry's working party. *Brut y Tywysogion*, the Welsh Chronicle of the Princes, describes them as 'a few chosen Welshmen ... in the absence of the princes'. This is usually taken to mean that they were not under orders but had taken matters into their own hands.

There was a fierce skirmish, and the fighting raged up and down between the thick woods, where the archers could barely make out their targets and the rough ground stripped by the axe-men, where fallen timber would trip the unwary and hard-pressed and bring them down, laying them open to the final blow from their adversaries. Many on both sides lost their lives that day, and soon the corpses underfoot made the ground, already slick with blood, even more treacherous.

Someone must have made it back to raise the alarm, for Henry led out reinforcements and almost joined the ranks of the dead that day himself, which would have changed the course of history.

Suddenly, one of the Welsh archers firing from a hiding place in the trees saw the three lions of the king's standard. Taking aim between the branches, and holding his arm steady, in spite of the hot excitement burning in his throat, he loosed his arrow at that most desirable of targets. His aim was true, but the king's man was truer. Hugh de St Clare, fighting at Henry's side, saw the danger to his sovereign and, without another thought, threw himself into the arrow's path, taking the fatal strike in his own breast. Perhaps this close call roused Henry to new efforts, and the surviving skirmishers were beaten back to rejoin the Welsh forces.

The tale of St Clare's bravery is matched on the Welsh side by that of Ynyr ap Hywel ap Moreuddig ap Sanddef Hardd. I'll call him Ynyr for short! Ynyr was luckier than St Clare and survived the battle, perhaps because he was fighting without his prince. However, he was so grievously injured, and lost so much blood, that his lord, Gruffydd Maelor of Northern Powys, was able to dip his fingers in Ynyr's wounds and draw four blood-red trails down his shield from top to bottom.

'Bear this as your coat of arms from this day forward,' said Gruffydd, 'in token of your bravery in this our cause, to hold Wales firm against the Angevin invader.'

And, indeed, according to the history books, Ynyr's device was changed to 'argent, four pales gules'. He also received another, more tangible reward for his bravery, as Gruffydd gave him the land and township of Gelli Gynan.

So many died that day from both sides that their bodies had to be buried there and then. Deryn Poppitt believes that the corpses were tumbled into the ditch, or fosse, of Offa's Dyke, bundling together enemies and friends without ceremony. Then the earth-work of the dyke itself was hastily broken down to cover them. This, he tells me, is why there is a wide gap in the Dyke as it crosses the valley floor and why the place is called *Adwy'r beddau*, the 'Gap or Gate of the Graves'. However, he still waits in vain for an archaeological investigation to be undertaken in search of evidence to support the ancient memory enshrined in the place name.

Henry's campaign, though not halted, was badly disrupted by the skirmish, which became known as the Battle of Crogen. The name, an old Welsh word for a steep sided narrow valley, survives to this day in the names of nearby farms, Crogen Iddon and Crogen Wladys. After the battle, 'Crogen' also became part of the Anglo-Norman soldiers' vocabulary, for they used it to mean 'desperate courage'.

Henry may have been desperate, but he was not beaten ... yet. He led his army further up the valley, still harried from its forested flanks by the Welsh bowmen and spear throwers. He followed the River Ceiriog upstream. Then he struck off north-westwards, up into the Berwyn Mountains, probably along the old, but still passable, paved track marked on maps as *Ffordd y Saeson*, the 'Road of the English'. It is known locally, especially to the elderly, as *Y Stryd Fawr*, 'The Great Road', and up on the tops it passes close to a mountain spring called *Ffynnon y Brenin*, the 'King's Well'.

Somewhere on the exposed tops of the Berwyns, looking out over the Dee Valley towards Owain Gwynedd's stronghold, Henry made camp, having avoided any further attack from above. Or so he thought. But while he kept a sharp lookout for showers of spears or arrows slicing through the sky, something much more prosaic was mustering against him. The Welsh weather was Henry's downfall. As recorded in the Chronicle of the Princes, *Brut y Tywysogion,* 'there came upon them a mighty tempest of wind and bad weather and rain'.

In other words, it began to rain. Then it began to pour. The sound of rainfall, merely a backdrop to life when you are comfortable inside your home, becomes an ominous auger if you are under canvas, as anyone who has ever been camping in Wales will certainly know. Henry's men had only the most basic provisions. They were now at the very end of an overstretched supply chain reaching right back into Shropshire, which was vulnerable to attack and pillage on every step of the packhorses' journey through the hostile territory of Wales. Deryn has ascertained, from equine specialists in the area, that the invaders' horses could have survived on heather if nothing more nourishing had been available. But the men, exhausted and hungry, had little chance to build their strength before the rain came, soaking everything they owned, putting out their fires and flooding their tents. With the rain came the wind, racing unimpeded across the high plateau of the Berwyns, which extends over three counties.

The common soldiers were in a wretched condition. But things were not much better for the nobles. Even the king himself was buffeted and blown, and could keep little comfort about him. At last, even Henry had had enough. He gathered the tattered remains of his battered army and retreated out of the wild Welsh hills and back to the comforts of Shropshire. His plans to subject the Welsh and annex their land to his Angevin empire had been beaten – by the weather. He lost his notoriously vicious temper. Once he had dried out, he marched south through the Marches to Shrewsbury, where he took out his frustrations on the Welsh hostages he held there, the sons and daughters of the Welsh nobility, including one son of Lord Rhys and two of Owain Gwynedd's. Henry personally supervised the blinding and mutilation of twenty-two young people. Then, his tail between his legs, he went back to Anjou and did not return to England for four years.

In the endless multiplication of war, Lord Rhys took revenge for the torture of his son by killing as many Normans in South Wales as he could get his hands on. But Owain Gwynedd, who had a reputation for 'equity, prudence and princely moderation', according to Gerald of Wales, reacted differently. When his remaining sons urged him to take revenge, he bade them leave the matter in God's hands, saying, 'By what they have done, they have alienated (God). He can avenge himself, and us, too, in the most striking way'.

As Gerald commented dryly: 'The English army, as I have told you already, learned what the wrath of God could bring.'

Henry's defeat at Crogen discouraged him and his Plantagenet sons and heirs from making any further attempts to subdue Wales. He later wrote of the Welsh to the Emperor of Constantinople in these terms: 'These desperate men could not be tamed, being ready to shed their blood in defence of their country.'

The courage shown by the Welsh at Crogen, together with the wiles of the Welsh weather, enabled Welsh independence to survive for another 120 years. This makes Crogen, if still a forgotten footnote in English history, an important event in the history of Wales.

Thanks to Deryn Poppitt and his colleague Mark Williams, there is a growing understanding of the significance of what happened at Crogen over 800 years ago, in the presence of that living witness, the Great Oak of the Gate of the Dead. More than seventy schools in Wrexham County Borough have been presented with a DVD made by Deryn and Mark. It recounts the battle, using both CGI and local re-enactors to bring key moments to life. There are now information boards interpreting the story in both languages of Wales. These stand on the path from the bus stop to the Great Oak and are easily visible from the valley road. On the bridge over the Ceiriog, a red and green plaque, paid for by the chocolate factory in nearby Chirk, commemorates the Battle of Crogen. The plaque was unveiled by Wrexham worthies in a cheerful ceremony in March 2009.

But there is a modern postscript to this ancient story, and it concerns the plaque. In the summer of the year that it was placed, Deryn took several groups of local history enthusiasts to see the bridge, the tree and the sites associated with the battle. In June, when the plaque had been in place barely three months, he was alerted to the fact that it had gone. It had been prised off the bridge, itself a listed structure. Deryn was sickened by what could have been either a wanton act of vandalism or the expression of still-smouldering nationalist rivalry in this most liminal of places. It felt like a wrong which could not be put right.

But later that summer, a lad from one of the cottages at Castle Mill was swimming in the river downstream of the bridge. He climbed out to soak up some sun on the southern English bank of the river. On this side, there is a pool which is over two metres deep, in sharp contrast to the swift shallow stream washing the other bank. It just so happened that the young swimmer was in the right place to notice the sun's rays picking out something red at the bottom of the pool. Had he been anywhere else on the bank when the sun penetrated the deep water, I doubt he would have seen the ruddy glint. His curiosity piqued, he dived into the water. Several times. At last he came up with something in his hands. It was the plaque, whole and unmarked. The vandals must have lobbed it over the bridge, knowing where the deeper water was and expecting it to disappear forever. But, like the story it commemorates, and the resilient oak tree, it did not disappear. Deryn checked it over, cleaned it up and had it replaced in its original site, fastened more securely.

'To get it off now, they'd have to take the bridge down with it,' he told me cheerfully, exhibiting exactly that quietly determined courage which made the name of the place he loves a by-word for Welsh resistance to oppression. Like the Great Oak, broken but not bowed, which remains a living witness to the events of 800 years ago, he will not forget the Battle of Crogen or its effect on the history of Wales. And nor will I.

14

A WREXHAM WEREWOLF

In the harsh winter of 1791, something strange was happening at Gresford.

Robert Jones was a smallholder who had a few sheep and a few cattle – just enough to keep himself and his family. He was on good terms with his neighbours, though he saw precious little of them, for times were hard and the working day was long. In particular, the farmer to his west, Rhys Williams, was someone he rarely saw.

Rhys lived alone, the only son of his father, from whom he had inherited the farm. He rarely came to market and then with his hat pulled low over his brow in order to avoid meeting anyone's eye. Horribly shy, he was more at home in his fields with his dog Mot than with other people. He managed his farm well, took care of his beasts and got fair prices at market. As the goodwives of the parish used to say, 'He minds his own business, so let others mind theirs.'

Robert knew very little about him really, although they had been near neighbours for years. He knew that if he needed help, he could go to Rhys and, according to the unwritten laws of neighbourly behaviour, Rhys would respond. In the same way, if Rhys needed help, he could come to Robert. But he never did. When trouble struck, it was Robert who had to go to him.

It was a hard winter, with a biting cold wind that blew the drifting snow into great heaps against the hedgerows and made life bitter for beast and farmer alike. It was a struggle to get to the sheep with fodder, and hunger made itself at home in their hollow bellies. But it was not only the sheep that starved. Some strange beast was woken in its lair by the cold touch of famine and went on the prowl.

Robert huddled by the fire late one November night, pulling on his boots to go out for the last time to check on the sheep before sleep. Bethan, his wife, wrapped a muffler round his neck and kissed the tip of his nose affectionately before standing aside to let him go to the door. Robert went out into the chill of the night and crossed the farmyard. He opened the gate into his first field and started towards the sheep huddled in the shelter of the oak tree. The snow-covered field was crisscrossed by sheep tracks, but in front of Robert, leading away from the farmhouse, were marks that brought him to a standstill.

Huge paw prints were embedded in the snow: they were like dog prints, but bigger ... much bigger. Larger than his own footprints, they brought him up short in shock. He looked around. There was no other sign of anything untoward.

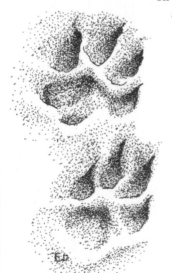

But Robert felt uneasy. Something was on the prowl, and the sheep, cold and stupid, would be easy meat. He looked across again towards the oak tree. The sheep there were placid and still. Nothing had harried or harmed them. But somewhere, a beast of some sort was roaming. He was sure of it. He made up his mind: something must be done. He turned on his heel, made for the gate and trudged down the snow-filled lane to the forge.

The blacksmith listened to his story, shook his head and said: 'I've never heard the like, Robert, but you're not one for making a fuss about nothing, so let's go to see what's what, will we? I'll get my coat.'

They followed the tracks for two miles, until they were on Rhys Williams' land. They were led to a scene of mutilation which made them quake with fear.

One snow-covered field was a lake of blood dotted with carcasses of sheep, cattle and even Rhys' faithful dog, Mot.

They found Rhys locked inside his house, in a terrible state. He wasn't harmed physically, but he was terrified. He had barricaded himself in after witnessing an enormous black animal that resembled a wolf ripping the throat out of his sheepdog. Then the thing had turned and seen him.

He had had to run for his life and had just managed to escape the beast, get back to his house and shut himself inside. He had bolted the heavy oaken door and hidden under a table in the kitchen, clutching the only weapon he had been able to find, a pitchfork.

Rhys, his voice shaking, went on with his story:

> The thing pounded on the door: Look! It's heavy oak, strong wood, but it was almost knocked off its hinges. Then … then the beast stood up on its hind legs like a human and looked in through the windows of the farmhouse. It was foaming at the mouth … but the worst thing was those eyes! Its eyes were blue and seemed intelligent and almost human.

Rhys shuddered. Then he stuttered out the rest of his story. After staring in at him, the beast had bolted from the window to wreak carnage on the farm.

Robert and the doughty blacksmith took Rhys back with them to Robert's farm, where Bethan settled the poor shaking fellow by the fire with a blanket round his knees and a bowl of hot soup in his hand. Robert went round all the neighbouring farms to raise the alarm, and bands of villagers braved the freezing weather with lanterns, muskets and pitchforks in search of the beast.

But they found nothing more. The huge tracks in the snow, the dead livestock, and poor Rhys' battered front door were all that was left to show it had ever been more than a figment of a lonely farmer's fevered imagination.

15

THE MARRIAGE OF OWAIN GLYNDŴR

Wales' great hero of the fifteenth century, Owain Glyndŵr, is closely associated with North-East Wales by his two strongholds at Carrog and Sycharth, and his battles against the English. But his particular connection with the County Borough of Wrexham is a gentler one, and his time in the quiet mere-side village of Hanmer must have been a happy and peaceful period for the man who was to become Wales' last fighting Prince of Wales. For it was in Hanmer church, dedicated to St Chad of Mercia, that Owain Glyndŵr married his life-long love, Marged Hanmer, mother of his many children and an ancestor of the Hanmer family members who still live in the village today.

Of the actual building where this happy event took place there is no longer any trace, for it has been twice obliterated by fire, once during the Wars of the Roses and again towards the end of Queen Victoria's reign. However, the present church stands on the foundations of its predecessors, and the view out over the tranquil waters of the mere, home to swans and Canada Geese, must still be much as it was when Glyndŵr stood waiting for Marged to walk up the aisle towards him. We cannot be sure of the date of their wedding, but it would have been around 1383.

Marged was probably born in 1370, though after such a long passage of time, this is another date which cannot be fixed with any certainly. She was the only daughter of Sir David Hanmer and Angharad ferch Llywelyn, and had three older brothers. The Hanmer family descended from Thomas de Macclesfield, who was given the parish of Hanmer by Edward I, partly as a reward for supporting Edward's invasion of Wales, partly to further Edward's strategy of creating a bulwark of supporters along the troublesome border between England and Wales, known as the Marches. Thomas' son changed the family name to Hanmer. It might seem ironic that one of his descendants should marry and bear the children of the last rebel leader against English rule of Wales, but a look at the Hanmer family tree will show that, though most of the carriers of the name were born in England, their wives were nearly all Welsh-born. This is a local example of the largely peaceful co-existence of Welsh and English on either side of a frequently redefined border, a peace that could be brutally shattered by bloody battles for control of territory.

Marged's father David, knighted by Richard II shortly before his death, was a Serjeant-at-Law, an English order of barristers which was the oldest royally created order, predating even the Order of the Garter. He became an eminent judge, a Justice of the King's Bench, and Member of Parliament for Herefordshire. He was an important man and undoubtedly highly respected.

Owain Glyndŵr was only about sixteen years old when his father, Prince of Powys Fadog, died. Fosterage was a widespread practice among the noble families of the land at that time, and was seen as a way to ensure that young noblemen had a chance to learn from and form close bonds with the friends and peers of their parents. Partly because of this custom, and partly because he was now fatherless, Owain was fostered by David Hanmer, though there is no record of the friendship that must already have existed between the two families. Owain probably went with David Hanmer to the Inns of Court in London, to follow in his foster-father's footsteps and study as a legal apprentice.

Dates and ages are hard to fix accurately for people who lived so long ago, but it seems likely that Marged was only a baby when the youth Owain first came to live at her family home. By the time he returned from the Inns of Court as a well-educated young man seven years later, she was still only a little girl. Their wedding probably took place in 1383. She may have been thirteen or thereabouts. Though it is distasteful to us today to think of a young man marrying a girl who was hardly more than a child, such marriages were commonplace in noble families at the time, serving to strengthen the bonds forged through the fostering process and create strong alliances between families. Often these marriages were not consummated until the girl had reached maturity.

It is impossible to know whether Owain and Marged loved each other when they married, or how Marged felt about marrying so young, but their pairing was a life-long one and survived the most turbulent of times.

Within a year of the marriage, Owain was far away on garrison duty at the troubled border at Berwick-on-Tweed in the service of the English King, Richard II. This gave Marged time to grow up, still living at home in Hanmer with her parents and older brothers. By the time Owain came back to Hanmer in 1387, in order to settle the estates upon the death of his father-in-law, he was an honoured and battle-hardened warrior, who had seen action in Scotland and Kent, and she had become a mature young woman. Perhaps now, after five years of marriage, they truly became a married couple.

Owain and Marged moved westwards from Hanmer to set up home on his estates at Sycharth and Glyndyfrdwy, and for ten years they lived the peaceful lives of prosperous landowners. Owain probably thought he would never see action in battle again. His court poet, Iolo Goch, described Sycharth in glowing terms in his poem 'The Court of Owain Glyndŵr'. He wrote of Owain and Marged's many children as 'a fair nestful of princes', and described Marged thus: 'The best of all wives … a bright lady of a knightly line; dignified, generous and of regal rule.'

Their calm life was abruptly ended when territorial wrangling between Owain and his neighbour, Lord Grey of Ruthin, flared into open hostilities. Then the flame of Owain's anger was fanned by the unfair response of the new King of England, Henry IV, to his appeal for justice. So he took justice into his own hands.

On 16 September 1400, Owain Glyndŵr raised his standard, his followers hailing him as 'Prince of Wales'. He attacked Ruthin, striking the first blow in what became a twelve-year battle for a free Wales. Marged's life, inevitably, was utterly changed. When Henry IV burnt Sycharth to the ground, she and the children fled to Harlech, where Owain captured the great castle built by Henry's predecessor, Edward I, and made it his stronghold. He held it for eight years and made great strides in his fight for a free Wales, establishing a Parliament at Machynlleth, setting in motion plans for a University of Wales and corresponding on equal terms with the King of France. Marged's role was that of Princess of Wales, though it is not recorded that she ever used the title, and she supported her husband and his campaign through thick and thin. But in 1408, the English stormed and recaptured Harlech Castle.

Owain and his oldest son Maredudd escaped, to carry on a guerilla war from the hills, but Marged had seen her husband for the last time. She and some of their children, including their daughter Catrin and son Gruffudd, were taken to the Tower of London, where they ended their days as prisoners of the English Crown.

This turbulent period, which was to change the course of history and make Glyndŵr's name one of the best-known in Wales, was all still to come on the day that young Marged walked up the aisle in St Chad's church on her father's arm. Surely, when they made their wedding vows, neither she nor Owain could have guessed at their destiny.

Marged died in captivity, and Owain's grave has never been found, so that folk tales have linked his name to that of the Sleeping King. This legend tells of a noble warrior, surrounded by sleeping knights and horses, who lies asleep in some hidden underground cavern until he is needed to defend the land, when he will wake and ride out at the head of his war band. None of Marged and Owain's children, as far as is known, bore children of their own, so that the direct line descending from them died out after only one generation. But the descendants of Marged's brothers still live at Hanmer, and the family name continues.

When the village of Hanmer celebrated the Millennium with a pageant about its past, Marged's wedding to Owain Glyndŵr was presented with as much pomp and ceremony as the departing twentieth century could muster. As the village website proudly records, the characters of Marged, her father David and her husband Owain were all played by members of their family, twenty-first century Hanmers. Members of the Hanmer family still live by the mere, and they still worship where their ancestors married, more than 600 years ago.

16

THE BOYS BENEATH THE BRIDGE

The villages of Holt and Farndon face each other across the River Dee, which forms the boundary here between Wales and England. A strategically important bridge links them.

The bridge is made of soft red local sandstone, and it had ten arches when Thomas Pennant crossed it in 1754. At some time, two of the arches were removed, and now there are five arches spanning the river, together with one flood arch on the English side and two on the Welsh side.

Bridges are powerful symbols of both separation and unity, and this one, joining land across water and linking two countries, has attracted its fair share of attention. The most obvious sign that it has been a bone of contention is that it has two names, being Farndon Bridge on the English side in Cheshire but Holt Bridge if you are coming to it from Wrexham County Borough in Wales.

According to Chester Archaeological Service, the bridge dates from 1339. In 1368, a court case was brought against the Earl of Warenne for changing the course of the river there and charging a toll to workmen for crossing the bridge, 'to the disinheritance of the Earl of Chester and the prejudice of his lordship'.

This part of Wales, being so close to the border, has had more than its fair share of trouble and strife. The bridge itself is the marker of a particularly unsavory episode in the grabbing for land and power which has plagued the region, and it is said to have been haunted as a result, since its very earliest days.

John de Warenne, the sixth Earl of Surrey and ancestor of the Earl of Warenne mentioned above, was one of Edward I's supporters in the battle to subdue the Princes of Gwynedd and take North Wales for the English crown. In 1282 de Warenne received, in return for his service, lands which had been part of the Welsh kingdom Powys Fadog: the districts of Maelor Gymraeg and Iâl. These were renamed the lordships of Bromfield and Yale, to emphasise that they had passed into English hands.

De Warenne's new territory included the Welsh castle of Dinas Bran, set on a hill overlooking the Dee Valley in Llangollen. However, it had been set on fire and partially destroyed by the Welsh when they were forced to abandon it in 1276. Rather than restore it, de Warenne began a new 'English' castle and town close to the ferry crossing at Holt, a strategically important border site.

Dinas Bran and the associated kingdom of Powys Fadog had passed to the four sons of Gruffydd ap Madog on his death in 1269 or 70. According to historical sources, these four sons were adults when de Warenne took possession of their lands.

All this is history, but now we move into story, for the events which are associated with the supernatural aspects of the bridge are difficult to fit into the known chronology of events.

According to legend, the two youngest sons of Gruffydd ap Madog were still only little boys when their land was lost to the English, and Edward of England made them the 'wards' – though perhaps 'hostages' would have been a more accurate description – of John de Warenne and Roger Mortimer of Chirk, another newly endowed English owner of land which had been part of Powys Fadog, the boys' rightful inheritance.

The two English lords now take on the attributes of wicked stepmothers in the old fairy tales. They looked at the young lads in their care and saw obstacles of flesh and blood between themselves and the rich lands of which they were only the caretakers until the boys reached the age of majority.

They began to plot how they might ensure that the lands granted to them by their king could be kept in their families and not have to revert to the Welsh heirs.

'If those boys were dead, there'd be no reason for Edward to return the lands to the Welsh.'

'Not while he seeks to subdue them all – the more of their land lies in the hands of English lords, the better pleased he will be.'

'Indeed, we would be doing him a favour …'

'Rather say, fulfilling our duty to our king …'

'Just so, you are right.'

'If something were to happen to them …'

'Yes, if something were to happen to them …'

So a plot was hatched, and the boys dispatched. It happened like this:

Late one autumn night, de Warenne and Mortimer rode back to Holt Castle from Chester. The boys were with them, each wrapped in a blanket and seated behind his guardian, both nodding drowsily, rocked into sleep by the rhythmic movement of the horses.

The journey was long and the hour was late. No moon brightened the night as the two conspirators, their minds made up to do the deed, carried the boys to their doom. As they traversed the flat Cheshire landscape, ever and again the waters of the Dee glinted beside them, for the track followed the twists and turns of the river to the crossing place they were making for, the bridge that led to Holt. The boys had been told that they would arrive there late, be put gently into their beds, and would wake next morning to find themselves back in the familiar setting of de Warenne's castle.

But this was not their true destination, and well both Mortimer and de Warenne knew it. A different kind of bed awaited them: the dark depths of the River Dee, where it rushed pell-mell through the arches of Holt Bridge.

When they reached the bridge, the two men urged their horses into the middle, then brought them to a halt. The boys stirred, but did not wake. The men slipped their feet from the stirrups, vaulted

down to the ground and turned to catch the boys as they slid from the saddles. The sleepy boys, if conscious thought surfaced at all, must have imagined they had reached the castle and were about to be carried up to their chamber.

But instead, without a word, both men turned to the parapet and dropped the swaddled bundles over the side of the bridge.

What shock, what terror must the boys have experienced, their limbs trapped in the blankets that wrapped them, their lungs filling with water, their desperate screams cut off abruptly as the swirling water sucked them down.

De Warenne and Mortimer waited only long enough to see their victims disappear. Then, with nothing more than a grim nod to each other, they remounted and rode on to Holt Castle.

People say that the screams of those murdered boys still echo beneath the arches of Holt Bridge on dark nights.

17

ROBIN RUIN'S RUIN

On Lightwood Green, the place where the gibbet pole once stood can still be seen on the eastern side of the common. Little did Robin Ruin think that he would end up there.

His story is a salutary one.

At the beginning of the eighteenth century, there lived in Overton parish a ne'er-do-well whom everyone called Robin Ruin, though his given name was Robert Lloyd. He was known to be a troublemaker and hard drinker, and his reputation for shirking and cheating had been quickly spread by the unfortunate few who had once given him a chance but never would again.

He knew all the local farmers by name and by habit, especially the well-to-do among them, though none would employ him since the time when he was supposed to be helping old Trevor Jones with the threshing but sneaked off to smoke a stealthy pipe in the hay loft in the middle of the day. Robin Ruin had fallen asleep and burnt the whole thing down and so acquired both his nickname and his reputation.

Robin drank in all the many inns of Overton, moving on as his credit with long-suffering landlords ran out. He kept his eyes peeled for opportunity and his ears open for any gossip or news that might be turned to his advantage without the need for anything as irritating as work.

He became interested in a certain Exuperius Williams, a prosperous tenant farmer on the Bryn-y-Pys estate. Robin's curiosity was especially aroused by the farmer's weekly trips to market, for he knew full well that Williams always came back with his pockets jingling. He hatched a plan to set upon the hapless farmer as he returned from market in the evening and rob him of the money he had made.

The day when Robin planned to enrich himself dawned bright and clear. Exuperius Williams set off early to market, while Robin was still sleeping off the previous night's drinking.

When Robin eventually stirred, it was almost midday. By the time he was up and about, and had made a few judicious enquiries to check that Williams had not changed his routine, it was partway through the afternoon. But there were still several hours to while away until the market was over.

Robin Ruin spent the time drinking at the Trotting Mare Inn.

Towards evening he set off to Overton Cross, hid himself in the bushes there and waited.

And waited.

And waited.

While Robin lurked in the undergrowth, he refreshed himself periodically from the bottle he had taken with him for just this purpose, and as the wait got longer so the bottle got emptier. Once the bottle was empty, Robin grew tetchy. He was not cut out for skulking in bushes, though he had in his time done quite a lot of it! He certainly was not temperamentally suited to hanging around half drunk, waiting to commit a crime. He grew morose, then frustrated, then agitated, angry with poor Williams for keeping him waiting …

Darkness fell, and Robin Ruin was on tenterhooks, for he knew that Williams would normally have been back by now. His brain was in turmoil, trying to fathom out whether he had missed the farmer or somehow been discovered. He feared that he was the one who would be caught in a trap, rather than the one who set it.

Robin had worked himself into a fever of fear and frustration by the time he finally heard someone approaching. Fuelled by adrenalin and alcohol, he came lumbering out of his hiding place and threw himself at the portly figure on the road, fists flying and feet flailing. His victim didn't stand a chance, falling at the first assault, and Robin punched and kicked viciously until the groaning figure was still. Then he crouched down and went through the pockets with the ease of long practice. He found a purse, but a quick heft of it in his hand was enough to judge that it was much lighter than he'd expected. He rummaged through the jacket, waistcoat and breeches, even pulling off the boots to feel inside them, but found nothing else.

Baffled, thwarted and, above all, angry, Robin Ruin took out his frustrations on the inert figure, before kicking him into the ditch and staggering away, not caring whether his victim were alive or dead. Or indeed, who he was. For, whoever he was, he was not Exuperius Williams.

On this day of all days, Exuperius had changed his routine. He had done better than usual in the beast market, and in conversation with a farmer from Chirk, found out that he had a fine pair of Welsh cobs which he might sell. He had felt both interested and prosperous enough to go back with the fellow to see the horses after market, and so returned home by a different road, which did not take him past Overton Cross that night.

Robin, of course, did not know this. He shook out and counted what was in the purse. It was nowhere near as much as he had expected, but it was more than he had possessed when he made the attack, for that afternoon he had drunk away every penny he had in anticipation of a better return for his efforts.

He was deeply disappointed with this poor result, and decided that the only thing to do was to drown his sorrows. Tired of the Trotting Mare Inn, he determined to go over to the Bryn-y-Pys Arms Hotel for the rest of the evening.

He settled down by the fire and began to drink his way steadily through the evidence.

But there was other evidence of his crime, groaning and bleeding in a ditch. And if it was not Exuperius Williams lying there, I hear you ask, then who was it?

The answer is: the landlord of the Trotting Mare Inn, whose name was Alan Sadler. He had also gone to market that day, being on the lookout for a new dray horse; unlike Farmer Williams, he had come back along the road past Overton Cross. In build he was not unlike the farmer, being tall and stout, though he was more advanced in years. However, anyone even a little more alert than Robin would have known by his gait that this was no farmer. Small wonder that he had so little money about him then, for he had gone to look and not to buy or sell. He had no luck at the market, and even less on his way home!

Poor Alan Sadler was unconscious for a long time – or maybe it was only a short time – and when he came back to his senses, he moaned in pain. He could not get himself out of the ditch and simply lay there, shivering and shuddering in shock. He was badly beaten and bruised, and every bone in his body ached. If he had been there all night, he might well have died of cold and exposure. But his groans were heard.

A group of estate workers from Bryn-y-Pys came along the road, and as they passed Overton Cross, one of them heard something that brought him up short.

'What's that, boys?' he asked, turning his head this way and that.

'What, Rhys, man? Are you hearing things?' joked his friend John. 'Hearing ghosts, is it?'

'No, whist now, listen!' said Rhys urgently.

Now the others heard it too. John went rather pale, suddenly afraid that it might really be a ghost, and regretting his words of a moment earlier.

Rhys had located the source of the sound by now and went unerringly towards the ditch. Looking in, he saw a darker shape in the darkness of the ditch. A pale face at one end, paler bare feet at other, the sound of a man in pain …

'I don't know who it is, but there's someone stuck down here,' he said. 'Come now, boys, help me get him out.'

With some heaving and grunting from Rhys and his fellows, and plenty of groans and cries of pain from poor Alan Sadler, they got him out and laid him down at the side of the road. John went a little way along the ditch, peering in, and soon found first his boots and then his coat, which they wrapped around the poor victim's shoulders as they helped him sit up.

Alan Sadler could barely speak, but by the moonlight they recognised him easily enough, for they all frequented the Trotting
Mare Inn from time to time. It was clear that something not of his
making had happened to put him there, and clear too that he was
in desperate need of warmth and treatment.

'Come on boys, this is what we'll do,' said Rhys. 'We can't get
him to the Trotting Mare – he's too battered to walk that far. Let's
take him over to the Bryn-y-Pys Arms. We can warm him up there,
and get Doctor Thomas out to take a look at him. I warrant he's
got a few broken bones and lost some teeth too, I reckon. Come
now, Alan *bach*, be brave. Can you stand now, boyo?'

They hoisted Alan to his feet and half carried, half guided him
to the Bryn-y-Pys Arms Hotel, where the landlord made up the
fire and his wife, tutting softly, brought warm water to wash the
blood from the poor victim's face and arms.

A slumped figure, half asleep, sprawled in a chair next to the
inglenook. The landlord gave him a nudge.

'Move over, sir, if you please. There's a poor fellow here who's
taken a right beating, and we need to see to him by the fire.'

Robin Ruin opened his bleary eyes, peered in a bad-tempered
way at the landlord and shifted over grudgingly to a bench by the
window, where once more he laid his head on his arms and, to all
intents and purposes, went back to sleep. But Robin was not quite
asleep. That glimpse of the beaten man had turned his thoughts
back to the violence he had committed so short a time before.

As Robin remembered what had happened, so too did Alan
Sadler. The warm water, applied without, and a tot of the landlord's best brandy, applied within, did their work and brought him
back to his senses. Little by little he told his solicitous listeners
what had happened.

'And do you know who it was, that set upon you so cruelly?'
asked the landlady, her voice soft with distress.

'It was so sudden I never got a look at him when he jumped me,
but when he'd put me down I did look up at his face, before …'
Alan Sadler's voice died away, as he remembered the sight of his
assailant's boot approaching his nose at speed.

'And did you know him?' she persisted.

'I did,' said Alan Sadler grimly. 'And I reckon half the parish would know him too. He's spent enough time at my inn and plenty of credit he's had there, true enough. Robin Ruin it was, and what has made him take against me, I do not know.'

'Robin Ruin?' echoed the landlord of the Bryn-y-Pys Arms, in a voice of rising intensity, 'Why, he's been in here since a little after seven. There he is – at the window.'

All heads turned to look at Robin Ruin, who was slowly – much too slowly – coming out of the seat and turning towards the door.

'Aye, there he is! The brute set on me and left me for dead,' cried Alan Sadler, in a voice hoarse with agitation. 'Hold him, boys. Don't let him get away!'

There was small chance of that. Rhys, John and their fellows dived on Robin Ruin before he could get clear of the table. They brought him crashing to the floor, held him fast and rolled him over.

'Blood!' cried John, 'Blood on his clothes – look!'

The blood, the look of dawning horror on Robin's face and the shouts of Alan Sadler when he realised that his tormentor was brought to bay all signalled that the game was up. Robin had not recognised his victim in the dark but did so now and cursed the luck that had brought him drinking in the wrong inn.

He was dragged down to the cellar and locked in there until the forces of the law could be summoned to deal with him. And deal with him they did. There was a trial, the evidence was conclusive and Robin Ruin, being already well known as a felon, was sentenced to hang.

Seemingly unmoved by his fate, Robin Ruin listened with no sign of emotion as the death sentence was pronounced and then leered at the judge with eyes that were full of malice.

'You've done the worst you can for me now!' he spat.

The judge turned his head slowly, slowly. He stared at Robin with a malevolent look equalling in menace Robin's own.

'No, I have not,' replied the judge. 'I further direct that your body shall be gibbeted.' And with this Robin was taken away to the condemned man's cell.

The sentence was carried out to the letter. After death, Robin's ruined body was taken down from the scaffold, his face and hands covered in pitch and his body encased in an iron gibbet, which was set to swing on the corner of Lightwood Green.

The gruesome corpse hung there, until the sight sickened even the most downtrodden of Robin Ruin's victims. But there was no mercy for Robin Ruin, and his body was left until it fell to pieces and went to the crows, the wind and the worms.

Robin Ruin was the last criminal to be gibbeted at Lightwood Green. Perhaps he was the last in the county. I could not find records of any other. But his story is not quite over.

More than 100 years later, in Victoria's reign, the land at the edge of the common was ploughed and chains from the gibbet were found in the ground. Some said that old Robin had been disturbed too, and there were reports of strange sightings and sinister sounds, so that people took to avoiding that way after dark.

In 1922 the framework of the cage was excavated and, with the basework of the gibbet itself, taken away. Since then, there have been no more reports of unnatural happenings. Does Robin Ruin lie quiet now at last, somewhere in the earth of Lightwood Green?

18

THE OLD UN
O' THE MOOR

Most of his contemporaries called Edward Edwards of Waen-Fawr
'The Old Un o' the Moor', and this name expressed affection more
than anything else. He was a simple man and always ready to do
anyone a favour, whenever there was call. Jane Evans compared
him to another man in the area by saying: 'The Old Un o' the
Moor is a neighbour; so-and-so is just someone who lives nearby.'
He was so gracious that the 'young uns' felt it would be a crime to
refuse to help with the hay making at Waen-Fawr.

No one would ever have thought he had once been young.
He was probably about fifty, but the children thought him ter-
ribly old. He looked a lot older when he took off his auburn
wig, revealing a head which was utterly bald. No one in the area
knew that he wore a wig, and this ignorance caused great distress
to the soul of one friend, who came from just over the border
in Llanarmon.

I need to explain that the Old Un loved to talk about boxing and
the strong men he had beaten when he was a young man. He was
telling the tale of these contests one day to Siôn, the Llanarmon
lad, and implied that he could still box. So the two had a go. It
seems that Siôn was a lot faster than the old fellow, and he succeeded in landing a blow on the Old Un's head, which knocked
off his wig. Siôn was horrified by this and ran away as fast as he

could to Jane Evans' house, where he blurted out: 'Auntie dear, I've knocked off the Old Un's head!'

Don't think that the Old Un's boasting came from a vicious nature, for he was not like that. In truth, the child in him never died, and this is why he always liked to boast a bit now and again.

The mountain sheep taxed the Old Un's patience and caused him great losses. His fields at Waen-Fawr were better grazing than the heather land and rushes, so the sheep would come, morning after morning, to devour everything in their path. They paid absolutely no heed when Sam the sheepdog was sent after them. It is easy to guess that old Sam was just as gentle as his master and had never learnt how to nip the heels of a few stubborn sheep. Somehow or another, though, Edward Edwards and his wife Elisa managed to live comfortably, in spite of the havoc caused by the sheep and the poor nature of the land. They won something worth more than all the gold of Peru, too, and that was the goodwill of those who lived near them. Any careful neighbour would be welcome to borrow the horse and cart when they weren't needed on the farm, and those same friends were ready to help out on Waen-Fawr whenever there was more work than usual.

One of his closest friends was Robert, Jane Evans' husband, and visiting each other in the evening was one of life's pleasures for them both. Edward Edwards usually went to see Robert Evans and his family before it got dark. For one thing, the people of Waen-Fawr usually went to bed early, but for another, the old chap was afraid of the dark. 'Well, friends,' he would say, 'it's time for me to go, before it gets dark: that way I won't get scared.' He was ready to stay later as long as he could have company on the way home, even though he only had a field length to go. Some mischievous lads knew of his weakness, so they went over to make a racket in his farmyard and insisted that they heard him say to his wife: 'It's better if you go to see what's up, Leisa.'

When he walked with Robert Evans to chapel across Green Lodge Mountain, they carried a lantern to light their path, and both families were of the opinion that the discussion on the way was almost as good as the service. Whether this could be proved would be a hard task, though it is certainly true that to journey is as pleasant as to arrive.

Like many of his contemporaries, Edward Edwards believed in ghosts, and he would talk of those he had seen here and there, and especially about the ones that come after midnight. Ned the Butcher was of the opinion that certain ghosts tend to appear at five to one in the morning. He had not the slightest fear of darkness or of ghosts either.

Edward Edwards had seen a ghost one time when he was coming home from courting Elisa.

'Where was it?' asked his listeners in worried tones.

'At the top of Old Gate Hill,' he replied.

'What kind was it?' they asked.

'One without a head,' answered the old fellow.

'Did you do anything after you saw it?' was the next question.

'Yes, of course,' he said. 'I said to it, "If you had a head I would talk to you".'

There is no reason to doubt the old man's word. After that, other people saw ghosts in that place, whether they were actually there or not. Didn't Jane Evans see a man sitting in the blackthorn? Some swore that there were terrifying ghosts around Thieves' Hollow every other night, but Ann Robert said that it was just Little Will from the pub dressed up in a white sheet, mucking about on his grandfather's pony. 'I know him well enough, night or day,' she said.

I ought to draw attention to Edward Edwards' talent for song. According to the evidence of those who could form judgments about that sort of thing, he had the richest bass voice for miles around and could read the old notation of music without much trouble. He loved hymns above all, and a sure way to win his favour was to spend time with him of an evening, going through the tunes and words that he loved. There was great pleasure to be had from singing, whether at Waen-Fawr or Jane Evans' house, and the old fellow was more in his element than anyone else there. It probably isn't true that when he sang bass in the kitchen at Waen-Fawr, the dishes would clatter in the corner cupboard, but it is true that no one could come close to him as a bass. If there is song in heaven, and a place for a dear old farmer with a bass voice, then Edward Edwards is as happy as can be.

19

LADY BLACKBIRD

When George Blackbourne came to ask her father for her hand in marriage, young Margaret was thrilled. George Blackbourne! Steward of the Trevalyn Estate in Marford, he answered only to Sir John Trevor himself, who was often away in London on Parliamentary business, so that it was George who controlled the fields, orchards, forests and workers of the great estate. What was more, he had right of residence in grand Rofft Hall. Why, she would almost be a lady! She would have a cook and a maid, a fine house and a happy life …

So Margaret told herself, as she dreamed away the days to her wedding. But it didn't work out like that.

The wedding was splendid, true enough, but the fairy tale did not last long after – certainly not ever after.

To put it bluntly, the man Margaret had married was a bully, a drunkard and a womaniser. He kept his bad habits hidden from her at first but soon ceased to bother to make the effort. He began to make trysts with other women, and to shout and rage about the least little thing, especially when in his cups.

Margaret was a good deal younger than her husband and much less worldly wise. Not knowing how to deal with his behaviour, she resorted to the conventions of polite society and pretended that nothing was amiss. However, when her parents came to visit, her mother noted Margaret's pallid face and nervous eyes, and shuddered at the abrupt tone Sir George adopted when speaking to his young wife, a tone which was all too similar to the way he addressed the servants.

'Daughter, tell me what ails you,' whispered her mother as they sat together sewing by the great window. But Margaret only shook her head, folded her lips and bent her face over her embroidery, lest her mother should see the colour rushing to her cheeks and the tears springing to her eyes.

When it was time for her parents to leave, Margaret choked back sobs as she hugged her mother tightly, and the older woman's tears flowed in ready sympathy. Both knew that something was badly wrong, but the conventions of life in eighteenth-century Wales allowed them neither the time nor the language in which to express their disquiet.

So her parents left and Margaret was alone once more … alone without being alone, for the servants who moved quietly here and there saw everything, though she could not speak to them of what was happening to her life, nor they to her. The husband she had thought loved her wanted only a trophy bride. Attracted perhaps at first by the unattainable nature of her delicacy and chastity, George Blackbourne had begun to tire of her gentle charms as soon she had surrendered her maidenhead to him on their wedding night and now seemed to despise the very modesty for which he once had lusted.

Over the next seven years, Margaret went through several pregnancies, but only two came to full term. Never robust, and weakened by her miscarriages and the difficult deliveries of the two survivors, Margaret nonetheless gave all she could to her children, who brought light and love into her clouded life, and on whom she poured the love and attention which her husband spurned. Crooning over them at night, or watching them at play in the nursery, she was able to forget for a time the loveless nature of her marriage in the delights of motherhood.

And though George lavished attention on the children when he was drunk, especially on the little boy who was his heir, neither his moods nor his treatment of Margaret improved; his infidelities grew more blatant, and his wife's frailty and her barely concealed disgust at his pawing led him to seek his satisfaction elsewhere more and more often.

Soon he had a string of mistresses around Wrexham and spent many nights far from the marital bed. Margaret grew angry and bitter, her face pinched and pale. She could no longer restrain herself from answering his drunken jeers with sharp words of her own. This, in the end, was her undoing.

In the early hours of a chill September morning, George let himself back into the house after a night in the arms of one of his paramours. He made no attempt to creep in quietly, letting the door bang behind him and clumsily bumping into furniture as he moved unsteadily towards the stairs. On the first landing, a candle in her hand, stood Margaret, dressed in her nightgown with her hair loosed for sleep, though it was clear from the tautness of her every muscle that sleep had eluded her.

George simply ignored her, pushing past her as if she were just another piece of furniture in his way, but she turned after him and grabbed his coat, pulling him round to face her.

'Where have you been?' she asked hoarsely, framing the pointless question of every betrayed wife. She knew very well the general, if not the specific, answer: 'With someone else, someone who lets me do what you will not.'

George said nothing, only grunted a little with effort as he pulled his coat free of her hands. But she would not let him pass and moved into his way.

'Answer me, where have you been? Why do you treat me thus?' Margaret's voice was raised now, her tone strident. George would not respond to such questioning – she knew this, but something had snapped within her and she was at last ready to confront him.

He stopped at this unexpected show of anger and turned to stare at her incredulously, swaying slightly on his feet.

'Do you dare to question me, madam? Who do you think you are?'

'I am your lawful wife and have been so these seven long years, and I will not suffer your shameful behaviour any longer!'

'Indeed so?' he asked, in a voice that was thick, sarcastic and suddenly dangerously quiet. 'And what makes you think I might care for your view on the matter? I have never consulted you about how I live my life, and I do not propose to start now! Finding no satisfaction here, I shall continue to seek it elsewhere. For you, *madam*, are the coldest excuse for a woman that ever a man had the misfortune to find in his bed!'

With these cruel words, he pushed her roughly to one side. The candle fell from her hand, going out as it fell and splashing drops of wax on the highly polished floor. Plunged into darkness, Margaret clutched at George's shoulder for support. Whether he took this as an attack or was simply more disoriented than she by dint of being drunk, he flung her off with great vigour. Margaret cried out as she was thrown across the floor, but her voice was abruptly cut off as her head slammed against the solid oaken newel at the top of the staircase.

Swearing loudly, George blundered towards her in the darkness, his intentions unclear, even to himself. When he stumbled against her groaning form, his anger was re-ignited. He grabbed her and pulled her to her feet. She fell against him, her head lolling. In fact, she was semi-conscious, but he took this as a sign of the passivity he found so infuriating. His rage flared as he shook her, yelling incoherently into her face, then pushed her violently away from him. Who knows whether he realised what he was doing, for it was dark and he was drunk: thrusting her away he propelled her down the sweeping flight of stairs to the ground floor. She fell from stair to stair, as limp as a puppet and already unconscious from the head injury. By the time she reached the floor of the hall, her neck was broken and she had stopped breathing.

George stood, panting, at the top of the stairs, trying to work out what had happened. There was a pattering of feet, and the housemaid appeared on the landing above, peering down with a lantern in her hand. When she saw the inert form at the bottom of the stairs, she gave a little scream, which she quickly bit back when George turned his bloated angry face up towards her.

'Sir, begging your pardon, what has happened?' she asked breathlessly, trying to bob a curtsey while staring down over the balustrade at her employer.

'Get back to your bed, woman,' he snarled, and she scuttled away, shaking.

George turned, without looking down again, and stumbled off to his bedroom, throwing himself down fully clothed on the tumbled bedclothes, still warm from his wife's body. He fell almost immediately into sonorous sleep.

The maid crouched in her room, ear to the door, until she was sure that he was out of the way. Still she waited, afraid of his temper, but at last could bear it no longer and cautiously pushed the door open. She peered around, then came out onto the landing, the lantern in her hand, and looked over the balustrade once more. In the gloom, it was hard for her to be sure of what she saw, but she made out a clot of darkness at the bottom of the stairs, which neither stirred nor made a sound. Fearfully, she went down. Her mistress lay sprawled on the floor, her head at an unnatural angle. Clearly she was past all help. The little maid shivered and snuffled, weeping into her hands, more from shock than grief. Then, not knowing what else to do, she crept back upstairs to her bedroom, and crouched sleepless under the covers for what remained of the night.

Morning brought light to the grim scene in the hall, but no clue as to how it had happened. The household gathered around the corpse of their mistress. George Blackbourne emerged from his bedroom, head still thick with sleep and drink, and peered down at their upturned faces.

'Madam must have slipped during the night,' he told them. 'I heard nothing. Did any of you?'

Averting her eyes, the little housemaid shook her head dumbly with the rest of them.

'Send for the undertaker. There is nothing else to be done,' ordered George. With that, he went back into the bedroom and shut the door.

Margaret's body was taken away and prepared for burial. Gossip ran like wildfire around the neighbourhood, but the members of George Blackbourne's household were too afraid of their master to speak of what had happened that night. George himself said nothing and was rarely at the house from then on, though he did have the decency, or prudence, to turn up for Margaret's funeral.

The main rooms of the house were closed up, the servants cared for the children and speculation was rife on whether he would leave the house and move away. But, much to the surprise of the good people of Marford, within six months he remarried, and installed the new wife, promoted from her former status as one of his mistresses, at Rofft Hall.

Once again, the Blackbournes became a principal subject of village gossip, with 'Poor Lady Margaret' mentioned over and over again. It was not long before the 'Poor Lady' made her feelings only too plain.

She began in the village, tap-tapping on windows in the dead of night. Those brave enough to peer out between their curtains saw an anguished face, pale as death, staring in at them. The unearthly figure, wrapped in its shroud, progressed from house to house, making its way towards Rofft Hall.

Margaret was going home.

Once she had entered the house, she climbed the stairs down which she had tumbled to her death, then worked her way past each room, moaning horribly all the while, until she came to the matrimonial bedroom. There she squatted down outside the door and kept a noisome vigil all night long, to the great disquiet of the room's living occupants. She left to return to her grave only as dawn broke.

This became a nightly occurrence, and even George was unable to pretend that it did not affect him, while the new Lady Blackbourne, after several hysterical fits, refused to stay in the house at all and returned to her former home, which, though much less grand than Rofft Hall, at least was not haunted.

Eventually, George, in some desperation, called on the priest of Gresford church to settle the unquiet corpse of his first wife. Success was only partial. Margaret's body no longer rose from the grave each night but her spirit continued to haunt the house and to wander through the village each night, tapping on the windows and peering in.

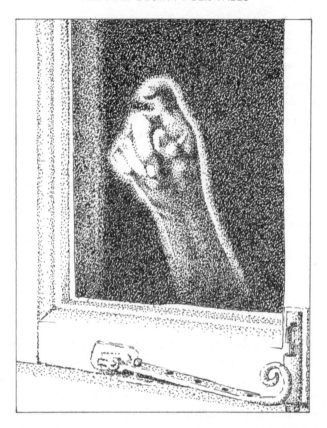

George survived her by some twelve years and fathered another two children on his second wife, but in 1725 he joined Margaret in Gresford churchyard.

Some people say that Margaret stopped wandering then. Others say that she still walks by night, and it is for this reason – to keep the village ghost away – that so many of the cottages in Marford have crosses built into the windows or walls.

Just as stories change through being told and retold, so Margaret Blackbourne's name has been corrupted over time. The ghost which taps on the windows and peers through them on dark nights in Marford is now called Lady Blackbird.

20

DANCING WITH THE FAIR FOLK

The fairy folk, or *tylwyth teg*, to give them their most common Welsh name, are known for their delight in the full moon. They celebrate its appearance with a *noson lawen*, or 'merry evening', of music and dancing. At midnight they rise out of their hiding places in the ground and join hands to make a circle. Then they dance and dance to their hearts' content until the first cockcrow, when they vanish once more.

To see the fairies dance must be a wonderful sight, but to watch them could cause your downfall unless you are very careful, very lucky or fortunate enough to have a companion with a level head and a piece of wood from a mountain ash. This is the one tree that the fairies dare not touch.

There were once two brothers, who had a carting business. They carried coal from Minera over the moor, and their business, though modest, was doing well.

Usually they finished work before it grew dark, but when the long summer days came, and it was still light well into the evening, they were tempted to keep going and to pack as many journeys into the hours of daylight as they could. What some-times happened, of course, especially if they tried to make one trip too many, was that they would be caught out on the moor as darkness fell.

One summer evening they were on their way back to Minera, the empty cart rattling behind their little pony and the full moon, almost as bright as day, picking out the pale track of their path through the heather. The going was easy and the air was mild, so they were both enjoying the peace of the night as they strolled along. Then one of them cocked his head and asked:

'Do you hear that, *boi*?'

They both listened. Faint strains of music were wafting over the moor. Intrigued, they turned off the track, leaving the pony to amble lazily onwards, until it realised they had lost interest in it, at which point it put its head down and started to graze industriously.

The two lads came to the edge of a little hollow in the moor, crouched down and peered over its side. To their astonishment, they saw a company of fairies dancing in a ring. They looked at the dancers, then at each other.

One had horror in his eyes: 'The fair folk,' he hissed. 'We must get away!'

The other had stars in his: 'Did you see her, Dewi? The one with the long red hair? She looked at me. She smiled at me. She's lovely, isn't she? Watch, here she comes again!'

Dewi was even more worried now than before.

'Gareth, *bach*, don't be daft now. Look away. Look away. Oh … no …'

He reached to grab his brother's arm, but it was too late. Gareth, his eyes fixed on the fairy dancer, was holding out his hand towards her. Immediately, she lunged forward and grabbed his wrist in her small but powerful hand. She pulled him over the rim of the hollow and into the dancing ring, grinning mockingly back over her shoulder at his brother as she did so.

As soon as he was enclosed in their circle, the fairies threw up a charm of invisibility, and every one, including Gareth, simply disappeared from Dewi's sight.

'Oh no! Oh no! What shall I do? What shall I do?'

Dewi, driven by this dreadful disaster into double diction, ran up and down helplessly on the edge of the hollow, not daring to step down into it, for he was sure that the fairies were still there, even though he could no longer see them. And if the fairies were still there, then Gareth must be too.

With this reasoning, he calmed down a little. He knew, better than I, how the fairies might be thwarted and Gareth rescued. He knew it would not be easy. But he knew too that unless his brother escaped their clutches before dawn, they would keep him forever, and he would be lost.

Dewi, calmer now and with some purpose to his actions, turned his back to the hollow and looked around the moonlit landscape. He was looking for a rowan tree, also known as the mountain ash. But although the moor was bathed in moonlight and he could see quite clearly by its light, he could not make out any trees standing tall against the bracken and heather. He quickly thought through the route back to Minera. He could picture no rowans on the way. He looked around again, more desperately this time, and then his gaze fell on their pony, wandering along in the moonlight, with its nose down among the grasses of the verge and their cart squeaking gently behind it.

The cart! Its wheels were made of rowan, which is strong and flexible, and a good wood for shaping. As far as Dewi could see, it was the only source of rowan for miles around. He led out the pony from between the shafts with trembling hands, before throwing the little cart on its side, thanking his stars that it was empty and he did not have to tip out a full load of coal before he could get any further. It was hard to free the wheel, and his anxiety about his brother made him clumsy in his haste, for he knew he only had until dawn to rescue Gareth. The fairies would not leave off dancing until the last possible moment, but once the first cock crew they would make away with Gareth, and he would never be seen again.

When at last the wheel was off, and the cart lay lame and battered on its side in the scrub, Dewi scrambled back to the edge of the hollow, clutching his only weapon in the unfair fight to win back his brother.

He knew that what was traditionally needed was a long branch of mountain ash, and at least two strong men to hold it out into the space where the fairies danced their invisible dance. This would allow the fairies' mortal captive to grasp the end of the branch as he was whirled by in the dance. Then his rescuers could pull him out of the circle, break the enchantment that held him and make him visible once more. Dewi was only one man, and what he clutched was a wheel, not a strong branch. But it was all he had, so it would have to do.

He braced himself against a stone which stood up proud at the edge of the dip, muttered a prayer, and leaned out into the space, holding out the wheel as far as his trembling arms would reach. 'Gareth!' he shouted. 'Gareth, *brawd*, brother, catch hold here! I'll get you out. Trust me, in the name of God.'

A hissing, spitting, bitter noise seemed to come from the air itself in response. Dewi shuddered, but he did not draw back. He stretched out with the wheel and began to sweep it through the air, still calling his brother's name, in a voice that came ragged and panting with effort.

Suddenly, the wheel snagged against something – something that wasn't there, or at least, could not be seen. Dewi stumbled, almost fell, but recovered himself as he teetered on the brink of the hollow. He planted his feet, clutched the wheel with both hands and began to draw it towards him. He knew that his invisible brother, spinning in the fairies' dance, had bumped into the wheel and now was clinging to it as his last resort.

Dewi pulled and pulled. Surely the fairies were resisting him, for the strain was enormous. But he knew that they could not touch the rowan wood and that if only he could pull hard enough, their grip on Gareth would be broken, and he would be free.

Suddenly something gave. Dewi fell on his back, the wheel thumping down on his chest and knocking the breath out of him. The wheel was heavy, much heavier than it had been. As he wheezed and gasped and screwed up his face, he couldn't work out what was happening. But when he managed to open his eyes once more, he saw, to his inexpressible relief, the figure of Gareth sprawled across the wheel. No wonder it was so heavy!

Slowly the two brothers extricated themselves from each other and the spokes of the rowan wood wheel. Gareth looked ruefully at his brother.

'You were right,' he said. 'She was no good. Oh, but she was lovely …'

'Never you mind about that now,' said Dewi sharply, 'Help me get this wheel back on the cart or we'll never get home. And mind you keep yourself well away from the fair folk from now on, though what they see in you I don't rightly know.'

And so the two brothers came safely home to Minera at last, just as dawn was breaking.

21

OFFA'S OFFSPRING

> There was in Mercia in fairly recent time a certain vigorous king
> called Offa, who terrified all the neighbouring kings and provinces
> around him, and who had a great dyke built between Wales and
> Mercia from sea to sea.

So wrote Asser, the ninth-century Welsh monk who was a scholar
and advisor at the court of Alfred the Great. His *Life of Alfred* is an
important source of information, not only about Alfred and his
times, but also about Offa, whose 'great dyke', a walled ditch, cuts
through the county of Wrexham, often in close proximity to that
other mighty earthwork, Wat's Dyke.

Asser lived only 100 years after Offa's reign, which lasted from
AD 757 to 796, and he is the nearest we have to a contemporary
chronicler of events. Do not, however, expect a historical account!
Asser had stories to tell, and, like most storytellers, he did not
let the truth get in the way of a good story. He gives a scurrilous
account of the deeds of Offa's daughter, Eadburh, which, though
certain basic facts can be substantiated from other sources, is surely
more folktale than history. I thought it was a good story to mark
the connection of the King of Mercia with Wrexham County
Borough, even though it does not mention the dyke ... In any
case, the dyke may have nothing to do with Offa at all: popular
belief in Wrexham has it that the dyke was actually made by the
devil, ploughing from coast to coast of Wales in a single night.

Offa was a powerful leader, and under his rule Mercia expanded its boundaries, until it was by far the most important of the seven Saxon kingdoms which eventually became England. By conquest and alliance he made his gains and so became a great king, for he was ruthless, ambitious and, as Asser implies, terrifying. It seems the women of his family were of the same bold stamp, for his queen, Cynethryth, was the only woman of the period to mint coins with her own image upon them, while their daughter Eadburh gained a place in Asser's chronicles because of her thirst for power.

Eadburh, like many women of royal blood of those times, married for politics, not love, and her union with Beorhtric of Wessex was undoubtedly part of her father's plan to secure his borders and extend his influence.

Offa helped Beorhtric to vanquish a rival claimant to the throne, by name Egbert, who was sent into exile at the Frankish court of Charlemagne. This put Beorhtric into Offa's debt, and from then on, royal charters in Wessex, as in Mercia, were issued in Offa's name rather than Beorhtric's. But Eadburh was no passive pawn in this game of thrones, and she relished the authority she gained as queen. Whether she loved Beorhtric or not, the story does not say.

As Queen of Wessex, Eadburh undoubtedly made her presence felt, and she quickly became a figure of fear at her husband's court. The servants soon realised that if she didn't like the way you looked at her, if she didn't like the way you spoke to her or even if she just didn't like the colour of your tunic, you could expect curses or blows. She had a vicious temper and lashed out whenever she felt like it.

She had enormous influence over Beorhtric too. Though his name can be translated as 'magnificent ruler', in fact he was a henpecked husband. Eadburh compiled a list of real or imagined slights she had suffered, and though she punished servants herself, when the offenders were of higher rank she demanded that the king pass judgement. This usually meant execution, sometimes exile.

On the rare occasions when she could not bend her husband's will to hers, Eadburh took matters into her own hands. Poison was her preferred method of removing troublesome men of influence, and this invisible weapon was deadly in her hands. It was not a happy time to be a thegn at Beorhtric's court.

Poison is a dangerous weapon, and even the most skilled hands can make mistakes.

Eadburh's husband had a young favourite, whose name was Worr, and Eadburh grew jealous of the time and attention which he won from her husband. So she decided to get rid of him. She prepared a deadly, but tasteless, potion and stealthily added it to Worr's goblet as he sat in the place of honour at the high table, between her and Beorhtric. She concealed her action with her long sleeve, while engaging Worr in animated conversation to distract him.

Then she sat back, smiled sweetly and raised her own cup, as if to toast him. Courteously, Worr lifted his drink, inclined his head to her and drank. Eadburh's smile became one of satisfaction.

But then Beorhtric leaned across and took Worr's goblet from his hand.

'Let no one drink my lady's health without sharing that pleasure with me!' he laughed, and drained Worr's cup to the dregs.

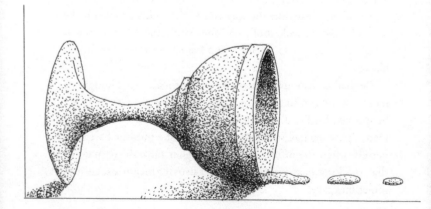

Eadburh's smile froze on her lips. There was nothing she could do, even if she had set her husband's life above her own, for the poison was swift working and she had no antidote to hand. In any case, she knew in her heart that she preferred losing her husband to losing her position.

Later that night the court was thrown into confusion at the sudden deaths of both the king and his favourite. Eadburh played the role of distraught widow well, but there were many who suspected her and few who trusted her. Enough rumours had gone around the court for the eye of suspicion to be fixed upon her.

She might have held on to a place at court and become Dowager Queen if she and Beorhtric had had a son and heir. But the eventual successor to the throne had little cause to love her, for the thegns agreed to recall Egbert from Frankia, and set him upon the throne. Egbert had been sent into exile by the combined efforts of Beorhtric, Eadburh and Offa, and she knew that the writing was on the wall for her.

She gathered as much treasure as she could – a significant amount, by all accounts – and fled to Frankia, there to throw herself on the mercy of the great king Charlemagne. It was as though she and Egbert exchanged places and fortunes.

When Charlemagne met Eadburh, he was attracted to her. She was a handsome woman, alluring and experienced. Power is attracted by power, and Charlemagne recognised power when he saw it. So did Eadburh.

But she made a bad mistake at that first meeting, which cost her a place at the court of the Franks, perhaps even the place at Charlemagne's side.

As Eadburh stood before the emperor, Charlemagne smiled at her and indicated his son, seated at his side.

'Now, Lady, tell me true: were one of us to offer you his hand in marriage, which would you prefer?'

Who knows why Eadburh answered as she did, for surely she must have known the right tactical answer. Maybe she thought Charlemagne was jesting, or testing her. Maybe she wanted to show how spirited she was. Maybe she didn't think at all, for she replied:

'Your son, my Lord, for he is younger than you, and will make a more lusty husband.' Charlemagne showed no sign of dismay, but his voice was steely as he responded.

'Had you chosen me, you would have had both of us. But, since you chose him, you shall have neither.'

Eadburh's last chance for secular power had disappeared, and her expression was shocked as she realised this. But Charlemagne was magnanimous and offered her power of a different kind.

'Very well, Lady, I will make you an abbess, that you may have your own domain to rule, and no men to interfere with your will. How say you to that?'

Eadburh had run out of options. She accepted.

She might have lived out her life in peace and comfort at the convent if she had been able to curb her appetites. Her lust for power could take her no further, but it seems she could not conquer lust of another kind.

She was caught naked with a lover, and Charlemagne personally intervened to have her expelled from the convent. It may be that the fact that the man was a Saxon concerned Charlemagne more than the fact of the sin. Perhaps he feared that Eadburh was plotting for power once more. Whatever her reason for taking the risk – and certainly hers is not the only story of a woman in holy orders ever to do so – the odds were now stacked against Eadburh, and she had nowhere else to turn. This time, she really did lose everything.

She ended her days, so Asser relates, as a beggar on the streets of Pavia in northern Italy.

How much of this legend is true is impossible to judge. It should be borne in mind that Asser was writing the life of his patron, Alfred the Great, whose grandfather was the very Egbert who succeeded Beorhtric. Plainly Asser had every reason to paint Egbert's opponents in as poor a light as possible.

It is certainly true that after Eadburh lost her throne in 802, the royal title Regina was not used again until Judith of the Franks, Charlemagne's great grand-daughter, became queen in 856. Kings' consorts after Eadburh were simply called 'the king's wife'. They were also prohibited from sitting beside the king at the high table.

Eadburh's influence on court politics continued long after she ceased to be a threat to anyone, just as Offa's dyke continues to keep his name alive in and around Wrexham, as the addresses of streets, *ffyrdd*, shops, schools and community projects demonstrate only too well.

22

SOME WONDERS
OF OVERTON

The yew trees in St Mary's churchyard, Overton, are listed among the 'Seven Wonders of Wales' in the old rhyme. There are reputed to be twenty-one trees, though some say the true number cannot ever be counted. There are inconclusive views about the age of the oldest tree, too, for though it is widely believed to be over 2,000 years old, predating the foundation of the church by some 1,300 years, there is carbon dating evidence that it is actually coeval with the church, being between 500 and 700 years old.

One tree that can be dated with confidence is the youngest of them all, which was planted by the present Queen on 10 July 1992, as part of the celebration of the 700th anniversary of Overton's Founding Charter. King Edward I established the village as part of his Marcher defences along Wales' border with England, and the grid-shaped layout of the streets is characteristic of Edward's defensive structures of the time.

The parish of Overton, of which the village is the centre, is shaped by a steep escarpment curving around the course of the River Dee. Several grand houses with estates stood at one time in the pleasant landscape of the parish, though most are now completely gone. One such was Bryn-y-Pys, home of the Peel family, who at one time owned many of the houses in the village itself.

Bryn-y-Pys was a large estate, which was built in the 1500s. It belonged to the Price family for many generations but was sold in 1850 to Edmund Ethelston and Anne Peel, husband and wife. Ethelston took his wife's name by royal licence, and by 1873 they owned nearly 6,000 acres of land in various parts of North East Wales. The estate remained in the hands of the Peel family until the 1950s, during which large portions of the land were sold off, as outgoings outstripped income. The house itself was let, but being by now in a very poor state of repair, it deteriorated so quickly that it was finally demolished in 1956.

The Peels, it seems, were always horse breeders and trainers: when they had only been at Bryn-y-Pys for nine years, they were instrumental in creating Bangor-on-Dee Racecourse. In 1858, two members of Sir Watkin Williams Wynn's hunt raced each other over the meadows at Bangor-on-Dee, and the challenge attracted so much interest that it was decided to make a day of it. The first Steeplechase meet was held in February 1859, the horses racing over much the same course as is still in use today.

It appears, however, that the Peels did not acquire successful horses when they bought the estate. Francis Richard Price, the previous landowner, met his stud groom one day as the groom was returning from a race.

'How did you get on?' asked Price.

'Came in second, sir,' replied the groom, a fellow named Goodhall.

'O well done, man, well done,' enthused Mr Price. 'And how many were in the race?'

'Just the two of us, sir.'

However, during their golden years as one of the foremost families of the parish, the Peels found themselves the proud owners of a wonder – one which is not mentioned in the old rhyme about the seven wonders of Wales but which has a story worth telling nonetheless.

The Peels owned a horse which was, and still is, one of only seven to achieve a remarkable feat: it won the Grand National twice.

Here is the 'rags to riches' story of a Cinderella of the equine world, the horse Poethlyn.

In 1910, Major Hugh Peel, a noted horse breeder, had his brood mare Fine Champagne covered by the stallion Rydal Head. The resulting bay foal was named Poethlyn. *Poeth* means 'hot', and *lyn* may come from either *llyn*, a lake, or *glyn*, a valley, though why the horse was given this name I have not been able to discover.

The foal was a pretty little thing, but Major Peel thought he lacked promise, for while Poethlyn was still unbroken, Major Peel sent him to Jones and Sons' Horse Sales on Eagles Meadow in Wrexham, where he was sold for seven guineas to a milkman.

Poethlyn was set to pulling the milk cart, and that might have been his lifelong fate, if a local trainer had not seen him when he was about two years old and advised Major Peel to buy him back. The major trusted his friend's horse sense and took his advice. He gave the milkman thirty guineas for the colt – which he had sold for seven! He also had to promise him the first salmon he caught in the Dee that year, before the canny milkman agreed to let the animal go.

Once the horse was back at Bryn-y-Pys, Major Peel made a gift of him to his wife, Gwladys, and they agreed to bring in a top-class trainer, Harry Escott, to see if Poethlyn really had potential.

They were not disappointed. Over the next five years Escott worked with Poethlyn and a number of jockeys, including Ernie Piggott, grandfather of the famous jockey Lester Piggott. Ernie was a champion rider himself too, as will shortly be shown.

After Poethlyn had won several races, Escott felt the time had come to try him out in the toughest race of all, the Grand National Steeplechase. The race is run on the National Course, which is over four miles long and features sixteen difficult jumps, all but two of which are jumped twice as the horses circle the track.

The Grand National has had its home at Aintree in Liverpool since 1839, but during the First World War, the course was taken over by the War Office and the race took place instead on Gatwick Racecourse, West Sussex, on land which now forms part of Gatwick Airport. It was a lot further away than Liverpool for a horse from the Welsh Marches, but Harry Escott felt that Poethlyn was ready for the ultimate test; in 1918 he entered Poethlyn at Gatwick on the third and last occasion that it hosted the race, which was temporarily renamed the War National Steeplechase.

With Ernie Piggott on his back, wearing the Peels' colours of yellow, with a dark blue belt and cap, Poethlyn made a fantastic race and finished four lengths ahead of his nearest rival, at the front of a field of seventeen horses. Gwladys Peel was overjoyed, and Poethlyn and his rider received a champions' welcome when they arrived back at the little station of Overton-on-Dee, horse and jockey alike having traveled both ways by train.

But more triumph was to come. In 1919 the race returned to its home at Aintree, and Poethlyn and Piggott entered again. Twenty-two horses started the race but only seven finished. In the lead was Poethlyn, making him one of only seven horses to date to achieve the feat of winning the race twice. His time was ten minutes and nine seconds. The betting odds on Poethlyn, at eleven to four, were the shortest ever on a Grand National winner, a sure sign that it wasn't only the Peels and Harry Escott who believed in Poethlyn.

There was great rejoicing at Bryn-y-Pys, as can well be imagined. The artist Sir Arthur Munnings was commissioned to paint a portrait of Poethlyn with Major and Mrs Peel. This painting, which still belongs to the Peel family, now hangs in the National Sporting Art Gallery at Newmarket.

Poethlyn and Piggott went back in 1920 to try for a hat trick. However, with rain falling and the going very heavy, Poethlyn was brought down by the eventual winner, Troytown, and retired from the race. Only five horses finished the course that year.

After this, Poethlyn's life took a slower rhythm. He retired from racing and spent twenty peaceful years at Bryn-y-Pys. In 1936 he posed a second time for the artist Sir Arthur Munnings, this time with the Major's greyhound, Bryn Truthful, which had won the Waterloo Cup in 1934. In 1937, Major Peel presented signed prints of this portrait of the two champions, standing in front of Bryn-y-Pys Hall, to every tenant of the estate.

Both Poethlyn and Bryn Truthful are buried in the grounds of Bryn-y-Pys Hall. A block of sandstone, engraved simply 'Poethlyn 1910–1940', marks where he lies, while a terrace of houses in School Lane is still named Poethlyn Terrace. At Bangor-on-Dee racecourse, once owned by the Peels, the Poethlyn Novices Handicap Steeplechase is still run every year in memory of this Overton Wonder.

23

THE WITCH OF PENLEY

Anne Ellis was a poor widow who lived as a lodger in the homes of others, making what money she could from knitting stockings and supplementing that meagre source of income by begging. In 1657 she was tried as a witch, accused by seven of her neighbours in Penley. Penley then was scarcely more than a hamlet, lying close to the border between England and what is now Wrexham County Borough and was then Maelor Saesneg. At the time, there were only seventy-one households in Penley, so the number of people, all from different families, prepared to go through the stress and strain of testifying against Anne in court, represents a significant proportion of the people of Penley.

What is the story of Anne and her powers, real or imagined? Quite a lot of the tale can be gleaned from the court documents, but some of the most intriguing details, after so much time has passed, can only be imagined.

In 1649 Anne Ellis was living in her own house with her young children. There is no mention of her husband, so it seems she was already a widow. By 1656 she was a lodger in Elizabeth Taylor's house and had a begging circuit, knocking on doors, which took her at least as far as Northwood, a little over eight miles away.

Her life was hard, and she did not make things any easier for herself, frequently upsetting her neighbours or cursing those who refused her alms. Being morose, taciturn and given to muttering under her breath, she may have deliberately cultivated the idea that she was to be feared, as a way of frightening support out of people whose sympathies were not aroused by her plight. Like many old women, then and now, she existed on the fringes of society and had no one to fight her corner for her.

The court depositions of her neighbours to Andrew Ellis, Esquire, Justice of the Peace, which were taken down in brown ink in June 1657, tell a sad tale of mistrust and meanness from both sides.

In 1649, while Anne still had her own house, Elizabeth Taylor's son Richard would come round to play with her children, probably quite frequently. Other people's children can be just as annoying as one's own, sometimes even more so. If Anne is to be believed, Richard upset her quite considerably on one occasion by urinating in her chimney.

'Curse you, boy, may you be lame and never walk well!' muttered Anne vindictively.

It may be that Richard did not even tell his mother what Anne had said, given that she carried on allowing him to go there to play. Nothing happened at the time, and Anne's words would have been dismissed as empty threats spoken in the heat of the moment if all had continued as usual. But it didn't.

More than six months later, Richard was again at Anne's with her children, playing outside at stoolball, a forerunner of rounders, while Anne was in the house. Defending the wicket – usually a milking stool hung up at shoulder height behind the batsman – he took such a swing at the ball with his hand that he spun right round and fell over. The others laughed heartily, but their laughter soon faded when it become apparent that Richard could not get up. When he tried to struggle to his feet, his left leg would not take his weight.

'Since that day,' swore his mother, Elizabeth, under oath, 'he has been lame and suffers great pain. She bewitched him, bided her time and then struck! My poor lad is blameless, and Anne Ellis is a witch!'

Elizabeth told the court another tale about Anne.

Anne Ellis had fallen out with John Birch, a thatcher from nearby Overton. Elizabeth did not remember what had started the trouble, but she did remember that John had then fallen ill, and nobody knew what was wrong with him.

So they sent to Anne Ellis to come to bless John Birch, that he might recover. And the old witch refused to do it! She has not a mite of Christian charity in her body. But John's daughter knew a sure way to find out the source of a curse. So they took a piece of thatch from Anne's roof, secretly by night, and this they burnt under John Birch's nose, that he might get a sniff of how it would be if the old witch went up in flames. Sure enough, he then recovered. If that is not proof that she was to blame, I don't know what is.

Elizabeth sat down, satisfied, though she still had one more accusation up her sleeve to level at Anne if she seemed to be getting away from justice.

Next to testify was Gwen Hughes, a labourer's wife.

More than four years ago, Anne Ellis first came to my door, begging. I refused to give her any meat. I had none to spare, and besides, I was nursing my Margaret then and so needed as much nourishment as I could get. For the child, you understand! Anne went away in some discontent, and the baby fell sick almost at once. Nothing I could do would ease her, so I asked Eliza Jeffries to fetch Anne Ellis to bless the child.

For four days she refused to come. For four days my baby suffered, shrieking most horribly and taking no food. Only when I was desperate, really desperate, did she come. She blessed the child, and straight away the babe began to mend. I have not trusted Anne Ellis since, nor ever dared to refuse her when she is begging.

Now my little Margaret is five years old, and as bonny a child as any mother could wish for. Or was, until Saturday last. She took and ate some of Anne Ellis' bread, and this made the old witch really angry. Margaret fell sick on the Sabbath, and by Monday there was a lump the size of a hen's egg beneath her arm. I asked Eliza Jeffries to keep company with me, for I was by now much afraid of Anne Ellis, and Eliza knows only too well how powerful she is. Did she not lose her own daughter at Whitsuntide last year, after she and Anne had quarrelled? The witch is a danger to us all! So the two of us sent for her to come to bless my child. As soon as she did so, Margaret began to mend.

But I dare not suffer the old woman any more, Sirs, for fear of what next may befall, so the next day I went to the Justice of the Peace and asked him, of his favour, to set out a warrant against Anne, that she might be brought at last to justice.

Gwen Hughes sat down, her face flushed and her arms wrapped around herself, averting her gaze from the old woman in the dock.

More and more witnesses added their voices to the accusations against Anne.

Margaret Barnatt's daughter shrieked pitifully until Anne Ellis was sent for to give her a blessing. Margaret herself admitted that when Anne had come to her begging at Whitsuntide, she had given her food, but it was 'not of the best'.

Edward Ffoulke's calf was ill and only recovered after Anne blessed it in exchange for meat. Susan Addams' cow was sick for three weeks after Susan's daughter refused Anne's request for milk. What was even more damning was that the daughter had seen a long-weaned calf suckling from that very cow near the house where Anne was lodging, and the cow began to weaken as soon as the calf was removed.

With so many fingers pointing the same way, it seemed unnecessary for Elizabeth Taylor to stand up again and bring out her accusations about Anne's behaviour on Christmas Day 1656, when she had at first refused to go to Susan Addams' house. However, after a greatly disturbed night, she had gone the next day, albeit reluctantly, and apparently healed a sick lad there. It seems as though Elizabeth wanted to make sure that every incriminating scrap of evidence against Anne was laid before the court, for she added this to her deposition. The atmosphere in Penley was rife with fear and menace, and the Justice of the Peace took the expected line. Anne Ellis was committed to the common gaol.

But she did not stay there. Sometime in July, resourceful Anne escaped and went on the run.

She was recaptured in Cheshire on 3 August at the house of a certain Roger Pottmore. When asked why she had escaped, she simply said that she was 'terrified with the apprehension of imprisonment', which seems a perfectly reasonable reaction. She also tried to implicate some of the people who had borne witness against her, saying they had persuaded her to run away.

On 28 September she stood in front of the Chief Justice of Chester at the Great Sessions at Flint, facing four charges of witchcraft, including that 'she did use, practise and exercise certayne wicked and divillish arts called witchcrafts, inchauntments, charmes and sorceries'.

She denied all the charges and somehow bailed herself for £200 to be of good behaviour. Who knows how she survived that winter or where she spent it, for she was surely shunned in Penley! The following April she appeared again at the Court Spring Session. To her mingled amazement and relief, both the Grand Jury and the Petty Jury acquitted her and dismissed all the charges.

Anne Ellis' fifteen minutes of fame effectively ends here, though there is one further mention of her in a list of paupers receiving the 'parish loaf' at Penley in 1670, so it is clear that she continued to live on the very margins of society.

How many other poverty-stricken and unsurprisingly cantankerous old women fell victim, like Anne, to accusations of witchcraft nurtured by ignorance, bigotry and fear? Although there was no equivalent in Wales of the witch hunts of continental Europe, and far fewer people were condemned to death for witchcraft in England and Wales than in countries where the Inquisition took hold, fear of witches and persecution of those who conformed to the stereotype were widespread.

Was Anne really capable of the magic she was accused of wielding? To the modern reader, her neighbours' accusations may seem laughable. Yet, however unlikely the premise from which prejudice and fear spring, the effect on their objects remains threatening and dangerous.

Penley is a small village now, and the sufferings of Anne Ellis and her generation have all but been forgotten. But prejudice against outsiders still dogs the descendants of the large Polish community in Penley, which was offered refuge, medical treatment and shelter there, for as long as they were needed, on the express orders of Winston Churchill, in gratitude for the support and suffering of the Polish Army during the Second World War. Penley's huge Polish hospital, which once had 2,000 beds, has closed now, and a small industrial estate occupies part of the site.

The Polish community here, in which children grew up speaking neither Welsh nor English but only Polish, until they went to school, is now dispersed. But the County Borough of Wrexham remains a popular destination for Eastern European immigrants, and the fear and suspicion which once attached to old women called witches is now all too often directed against 'foreigners', some of whom were in fact born in Wales, even though their mother tongue is not 'the language of heaven'.

Human nature is slow to change.

24

THE PIG OF THE VALLEY:
JOHN ROBERTS THE CUNNING MAN

John Roberts was a Cunning Man. He lived to a great age, being born in 1716 and dying at the age of ninety in 1806, and he built a great reputation during this long and eventful life. Like others of the Cunning Folk, he could read your mind, tell your fortune, dismiss your troublesome ghost and give you a charm for love or good luck ... as long as the price was right. His home was in the village of Penycae, and people travelled from far and wide to consult him.

He was known as *Mochyn y Nant*, 'the Pig of the Valley', which is the name by which he is best remembered. This nickname may have been a reference to the state of his home, which was described as having a 'forlornness and an ancient tarnish' by Thomas de Quincey. The writer, famous for his *Confessions of an English Opium-Eater*, came to Penycae as a seventeen-year-old to have his fortune told by John Roberts in 1802.

Like de Quincey, most people who sought his advice came to Penycae, but John Roberts could be called on to make home visits if the rewards were sufficiently tempting. So it was that he once travelled south, to the valley of the River Towy, in response to a desperate request from a moneyed lady for his help.

As soon as he arrived she regaled him with an account of her troubles:

My dear departed sister, God bless her soul, left me three precious jewels in her will. I treasure them, not only for their own worth, though they are fine, but for her memory. I have never had them set, nor worn them, but kept them always safely closed away in a casket in my chamber. But they have gone! Disappeared! Sir, if, by your powers, you can bring them back to me, I will pay you the princely sum of £50. Now tell me true, can you help me?

To be honest, John did not pause to wonder if he were up to the job or not. Fifty pounds was far too tempting an offer to be turned down, and whether he could do it or not, he was very hopeful of somehow obtaining the reward.

'Indeed I can, dear lady, and you have made a wise choice to call on me. I will be happy to help you on the terms you offer. Of course, I prefer payment in advance.'

This was not altogether to his would-be employer's taste, for though she was desperate for help, she was canny enough when it came to spending money. 'Fifty pounds is a lot of money. I feel it would not be unreasonable of me to ask for proof of your powers first. Will you agree to a test?'

John was not keen on this idea but could see no way to refuse. The lady left him sitting there and returned after a few minutes with a small, ornate wooden chest in her hands.

'This is the jewellery box in which I have always kept the gems which are lost. They are not there now, more's the pity, but something else is. Can you tell me, sir, without opening or touching the box, what is now inside it?'

John looked at the box. He longed to pick it up, give it a shake and prise the lid open. But his potential employer kept a firm hold on it, though she did extend it towards him, a searching look in her eyes.

He had no idea what was in there, nor could he think of any way to find out. The prize was slipping away from him. Regretfully, the Pig of the Valley could see nothing to do, apart from confessing his ignorance. 'There is no hope for the Pig,' he murmured ruefully.

His inquisitor stared at him, admiration replacing astonishment on her face.

'Sir, I was wrong to doubt you. Well done, sir! Oh, very well done!'

With that, she opened the lid of the box. Inside was a piece of salt pork, snatched from the larder as she searched for the most unlikely thing that might ever be found in a jewellery box.

Needless to say, John only smiled modestly and shrugged his shoulders as if to imply that his powers were beyond question. The money immediately changed hands and, full of respect, John Roberts' new employer asked whether he needed anything to help him carry out his magical investigations.

Flushed with unexpected success, greedy John, 'the Pig', said: 'Yes, I will need not one, not two, but three good meals brought to me, so that I can build up the strength required for my magic.'

His grateful employer hurried away to order the first meal and arrange for a room to be prepared, where John Roberts might eat and gather his forces in peace.

He had not long been ensconced in the room, with his thoughts darting to and fro between anticipation of the delicious meal and perplexity about how to justify it and its successors, when a footman arrived with a steaming salver.

The servant lifted the silver lid covering the dish and John Roberts sniffed appreciatively.

'Ha, I have the first!' he murmured, as the man set down the dish.

The footman stiffened in horror at these words. Rumours of John Roberts' magic had raced around the house, and everyone had heard of his success in their mistress' test. Most of those below stairs were agog to see the famous Pig of the Valley. But this man had been dreading such a meeting. He was the one who had stolen the gems, with the help of two accomplices also in the rich lady's employ, and now he feared to be unmasked. John's greedy words on seeing the meal held quite a different meaning for the thief standing in front of him. In confusion and some fear, the footman bowed, attempting to shield his face, and with an almost inaudible mutter left the room as quickly as he dared.

John hardly noticed the man's discomfiture, for his whole attention was devoted to the feast before him. He packed it away, reflecting with satisfaction that even if he had to return the cash, at least the food would be beyond recall. Then, in need of a rest, he stretched out on a couch to aid digestion with a nap.

An hour or so later, he was woken from a pleasant dream by a gentle tap on the door.

'Come in,' he called imperiously, and a different footman came in, carrying another meal. The first servant, too terrified to face John Roberts a second time, had insisted that one of his fellows take his place.

The man set down and uncovered the dish, held a chair for John, and finally placed himself unobtrusively behind the chair, out of sight, but where he could watch John and try to make him out. For this was another of the thieves, and he had a lively interest in understanding whether his friend's fears of John and his powers were justified. John Roberts scoffed down his food. 'Perhaps, after all,' thought the thief, 'this is why he is known as "the Pig of the Valley".'

Pushing the empty platter away with a sigh, John settled back and clasped his stomach appreciatively.

'That's the second in the bag, anyway,' he murmured contentedly, reasoning that food in the belly was worth more than gold in the hand, which might soon have to be returned.

But to the thief, John's meaning seemed quite otherwise. He was discovered! As sure as could be, the Cunning Man was on the trail of the thieves. Or so the footman thought. And so he said to his two partners in crime, back below stairs, John's cutlery clattering against the empty plate in his shaking hand. The conspirators muttered together, in fear and trembling. When the third meal was ready, the last man squared his shoulders decisively.

'I'll take the food,' he said, 'and if he really does know we're guilty, I'll confess and put myself at his mercy. We should promise to give him the jewels if he will agree not to give us up. Better to lose the loot and keep our jobs, than be thrown into jail.'

The others shuddered at the thought and agreed. Pocketing the gems and grasping the steaming silver salver, the third man set off upstairs.

He knocked and, at John Roberts' command, opened the door and walked in.

'Ah, here's the third. I've got the lot!' cried John triumphantly. Imagine his surprise when, setting down the dish rather suddenly, the white-faced footman fell to his knees and began to gabble out a full confession and a plea for forgiveness, at the same time tipping three gems out onto the table in front of John.

'Take them, sir, take them, and restore them to our mistress. But I beg you, do not reveal our names. If you do, we will rot in prison for the rest of our lives. Spare us, and we will make sure that you are well fed whenever you come here.'

John composed his features into an appropriately stern expression.

'You have committed a dreadful crime, which my magic had revealed to me. But you and your fellow villains do well to throw yourselves on my mercy. I will ensure that the jewels are returned, in such a way that suspicion does not fall on you. Yes, I am merciful, and your promise to see me well fed has softened my heart towards you. Now, go! And tell the other thieves of our agreement.'

The man scuttled away, leaving John Roberts to enjoy his meal, its flavour subtly enhanced by the bright gems beside his plate. When he had eaten his fill, he picked up the jewels and turned them over and over in his hand, wondering how to get them back to their owner without giving away the thieves. The sound of fowl in the yard outside gave him an idea. He went out, 'to take a turn in the air', as he informed the lady of the house when she came bustling up to ask whether he had yet solved the mystery.

'You shall not have long to wait, madam,' said John, sweeping past her into the yard. 'Now, I pray, leave me in peace: I must commune with the spirits of the air.'

What John meant by 'spirits of the air' was not ethereal beings, but rather the hens, ducks and geese, which filled the yard with flurries of flutters and feathers and a cacophony of clucking, quacking and honking: not much peace to be had there!

But this was exactly what John wanted. Under cover of the confusion, he approached the largest goose, and before it knew what was happening, he tucked it under his arm and forced open its beak, in one swift movement. He pressed in the three gems and held the beak shut, all the while stroking its throat, until the unfortunate bird had swallowed the unwanted morsels. As it bustled away, honking in disapproval, he made his way back to his employer, who had been standing in the doorway to the yard all this time, watching him in some confusion, unable to see what he had done to the goose while it was under his arm.

'There is one more meal to be had,' he said to her, 'And this time you must share it with me, for it is then that the whereabouts of the missing gems will be revealed. Have them kill and roast the goose I picked up, and make sure it is no other goose but that one. When we sit down to eat, you will have the final proof of my power.'

When the three guilty footmen, their faces pinched and pale, brought the roast goose, with all its accompaniments, to the table, John Roberts made great play of sharpening the knife, before beginning to carve the goose. He cut into the crop and triumphantly brought out the gems he knew were inside.

The lady's face brightened, and the conspirators regained their colour, as the Pig of the Valley spun a long arcane tale to explain how the goose had swallowed up the gems, and how he, mighty conjuror that he was, had discovered them.

John Roberts made a fine profit, in both gold and grub, from his excursion to the Towy valley and won the undying gratitude of a fine lady as well as her three footmen. They were so impressed by the Pig of the Valley's clairvoyance that they never dared to venture outside the law again, in spite of the fact that he was over 100 miles away, safe home in Penycae with his fifty pounds, the memory of four good dinners and a healthy appreciation of the good fortune which had enabled him to keep the secret of his 'magic powers' and win the day.

25

BURIED ALIVE FOR
EIGHT DAYS

Browsing through old copies of *The Rhos Herald* in Wrexham's A.N. Palmer Centre for Local Studies and Archives, I came across the extraordinary story of what had happened to Mr Samuel Lewis as a twelve-year-old boy. Over three weeks in April and May 1932, the paper serialised a sensational tale from Samuel's youth, told in his own words. I would be hard put to better his version, so I have chosen to reproduce it here in full, under the *Herald*'s attention-grabbing headline: 'Buried Alive For Eight Days'.

This is the story of my experience as a collier boy, when I was entombed with another man, Daniel Jones, Rhos, in a colliery close to my home for eight days. This happened on 23 April 1868. It was in the year 1867 that I first began to work as a colliery boy. I did not like it at first, but was soon broken in, and continued until this memorable accident occurred, when I was twelve years and eight months old.

I was not supposed to go to work on this particular morning, as arrangements had been made for me to do our gardening. However, I was first to be up in the morning, to seek for work, but was promptly told to go back to bed, which I obeyed. Soon after my brothers had gone, I got up again, and prepared to seek for work. Before going, I called my mother and said, 'I am going to see if I can have work,' and she replied, 'No, don't go,' several times. 'Mother,' I said, 'I will not be long if I find there is no work. Should you have any broth or soup, I would prefer it to having tea if I get work,' and the last words I heard my dear mother say was, 'Don't go.'

But I disobeyed her.

That was a bad start the first thing in the morning, which made me very unhappy and guilty. But more was to come, and the way of transgressors is hard.

Well, I arrived at the Colliery on a cloudy heavy threatening morning: I was told that two boys were wanted. There were several boys beside myself seeking work, and to decide who should work, lots were drawn. The manager, Mr George Valentine, held in his hand pieces of straw and the boy who drew the longest piece was given work. Anyway, I was successful.

The cage in which we were to descend did not come up to the top, as usual, owing to alterations below, so I was helped on to the cage by Daniel Jones, whom I was to help. On our journey down I could hear the sound of a mighty river, which made me quake with fear.

When the cage stopped, I saw that the usual platform had been washed away, and two streams of water were flowing into the sump, causing a loud roar. With the assistance of Daniel Jones I safely crossed two beams to get from the cage to the road, by a narrow way, owing to timber being put crossways to keep the top safe, and only sufficient way for a man to go through.

Once inside, I could quite understand the reason: the timbers for about twelve yards were all broken in the centre, owing to tons upon tons of rubbish and stone weighing heavy upon them, which caused the coal wagons to roof as they came along, and made those who had to put them on the cage very angry and brought forth very unparliamentary language!

It was this problem that caused the Company to lower the platform, and we could hear this operation from our working place.

My mother by now had sent my breakfast of soup and bread and butter. I had after my breakfast one and a half pieces of bread and butter left in my breadbox.

Whilst chatting together before restarting work, we heard a loud report like thunder, which shook the place were we sat: we immediately ran to see the cause, and to our horror, right before our eyes the aperture where we came in was blocked with debris, but how far up from where we were, of course, we could not say. It happened so quickly and completely that there was no room for escape.

It was a terrible ordeal when we recognised our predicament. My comrade Daniel wept bitterly, mentioning his Granny. Now about myself: you are aware how I disobeyed my dear mother whom I loved so much, just a few hours before, and now, in agony of despair of ever seeing her again, I imagined hearing that warning: 'Don't go'. It haunted me, and I cried more and more.

Oh! That I had listened to mother: I would not be imprisoned here, and I felt sure she was breaking her heart with grief, owing to my disobedience, and suffering terrible agony of soul.

Occasionally Daniel would give a loud shout, hoping to be heard by rescuers, he also knocked hard on a disused door in the hopes of being heard. We listened intensely, but all that met our ears were the falls of earth and the cracking of the timber.

We sat in an empty tub, crying and sobbing. For some time not a word passed between us. The silence was at last broken by Daniel suggesting that we should explore some old workings, to see if we could get to the shaft which was opposite us. I pleaded with Daniel that it would be useless to venture, as I knew the place very well, and knew no one could get through such great obstacles. Still, I considered the attempt, for the sake of my friend Daniel. We prepared to go out and explore the old workings. Daniel took several candles with him and I carried an oil lamp.

The attempt we made was very risky: for about twenty yards or so the road was bad, the timbers on each side had fallen one against the other in a zigzag fashion. We had to make our way as best we could, crawling in a stream of water. I went behind Daniel, afraid in my heart of him disturbing the timber as he struggled along. He was a well-built man, and it was a difficult task. I can tell you, we were very glad to get safe through and to be able to stand upright again. We now had a clear road for a long stretch until we came to a big fall. It so happened there was an opening, which enabled us to climb over large boulders of stone, until we came to an aperture.

There was just sufficient room for Daniel to get into this entrance. It was full of water up to Daniel's armpits, so he had to carry me with his arms above his head through the deep waters. Presently we came to a place we always called 'The Parting'. It was here that we all used to have our meals, and it recalled to me memories of the fun and hilarity we used to enjoy together.

After a short rest, Daniel and I continued our journey until we reached the place I quoted as impossible to get through. I pushed myself in through the narrow opening until I could get no further. Neither could I get back. I was wedged in. Daniel had to pull me out by my legs. I tried to dig a way with my hands until my fingers were sore, but only a rabbit could have managed to burrow through.

We had to retrace our steps to where we started, in a very disconsolate mood. Poor Daniel was overcome with grief, and as we came along and saw the lighted candles we had left, he wept. Once again Daniel took me in his arms and carried me through the deep waters and put me safe through the aperture.

We now went a long way in another direction until we guessed we were somewhere near the shaft. Here we rested. Daniel thought that if he shouted someone might hear him, but although we both shouted loud, there was no reply. Daniel fell on his back in an agony of despair. I also sobbed bitterly, for it seemed hopeless to expect anyone to rescue us.

By and by, we felt better, and made our way to the main road. Here we had to crawl out, as we did at the start, through water from that zigzag tumbledown tunnel. Our clothes got very wet and we had to take them off, wring them and dry them as best we could.

The next important thing to do was to seek a dry place where we could make a place of rest. For this purpose we selected the donkey's stable, which was quite clean and tidy. I now remembered that I had left in my food box one piece and a half of bread and butter. I gave Daniel the whole piece and ate the half piece myself, not knowing we should be imprisoned so long.

We were now very silent. I was on my knees, trying to pray, so also was Daniel. The lighted candles were getting dim by now, owing to bad air.

Daniel suddenly turned to me and said, 'I have been praying that we both should die.' That broke my heart, and I told him that I was praying to live, as I wanted to see my mother. I had not been happy in my mind owing to my disobedience. God knew how sorry I was, and, young though I was, before long I had that peaceful resignation to die if that would be his will. Still, my mind and heart wandered home as I lay by that tub, recalling how I had spent the previous Sunday evening with a boy who was my chum, and how we sang some Welsh hymns for his grandfather.

We sat there with twelve candles, which eventually all went out and left us in darkness.

I then laid myself down to sleep. I had a pillow of stone and pebbles. Daniel gathered a little hay and covered my legs, very thoughtfully shielding me with a donkey collar. These helped me to keep warm, and with Daniel's coat over me I was very cosy, under the circumstances. So we slept, but for how long I do not know.

In my dreams, I thought I was at home in bed. When I became fully awake, I realised where I was. I laid myself down again, brokenhearted and sad. Daniel wanted to know what the matter was and I told him about my dream.

'I think,' said Daniel, 'you had better come with me for a walk.'

So we went quietly in the darkness up an incline for a good way. We made it our business to visit the shaft where the tub was, and I again went on my knees to pray, in my boyish way, for deliverance. Daniel also prayed silently and told me that this time he had prayed that we should live. I told him how glad I was to know that, because I wanted to live.

In our life down in the dark workings my soup can came in very handy to carry water, as did Daniel's tin bottle. I appointed myself the water carrier. Breathing now became difficult and at times I laid myself flat on the ground with my head right on top of the water, for I found this eased my breathing. In this way our life continued.

Then one day as I made my way as usual to fetch water I beheld a light in the darkness, but could not see anyone. I was not frightened, but filled with an unspeakable joy!

When I got nearer I found that the light was a reflection through a crack in the roof. I heard no sound or human voice, nor did I try to make myself heard. I made as much haste as possible to reach Daniel and tell him that our rescuers had come.

'Daniel,' I said, 'they have come to rescue us. We are saved.'

Daniel looked at me and said, 'No, you are fancying things.'

Again I repeated, 'They have come for us.'

Daniel again replied, 'No, my boy, it is only your heart beating.'

'No, no,' I said persistently, 'I saw a light.'

'Well,' said Daniel this time, 'I will come for a walk with you and see for myself.'

Daniel was still full of unbelief until we arrived at the place where I had seen the light. Then he believed and was overjoyed.

He at once called out, 'Hello, lads.'

They answered, 'Hello, there! Are you alive?' As if they could not believe.

I thought I heard someone shout, 'Hurrah' and 'Thank God.'

'Is Sammy alive?' called a voice.

'Yes,' replied Daniel.

Daniel then asked me to go back and fetch some of the candles, which were left down the road. I went, but could not find them in the darkness, and in my weakness and excitement, I collapsed.

During this time our rescuers had made an opening to reach us. Daniel was the first to be rescued, and as I came to myself, I heard someone asking, 'Where is Sammy?'

'Tell us the truth, Daniel,' went on the voice, 'Is he alive?'

'Yes,' said Daniel, 'he is alive."

Some of the rescuers attempted to come through the opening to us, but were driven back by the foul air. I had by now come within a few yards to the opening, just when Daniel was about to seek for me. I presented myself at the opening, and when they saw me alive and in the flesh, these brave men kissed me until my face was wet with their tears of joy.

My first enquiry when I breathed the fresh air was: 'Where is my dear mother?'

We were now lifted from the shaft, where we were, to the main shaft, where preparations for our comfort had been made until we could be brought to the surface, and the medical doctor came along with restoratives.

I now had a glance upwards to see how far the pit had come down, and I noticed we were not far from the rock, which held the upper portion intact. It was this that saved our lives, for had it been otherwise, we should have been doomed.

Eventually we were taken up and placed in a cabin where there was a good fire. I had to close my eyes, as the light was too much for me to bear after being in darkness so long.

I wanted to walk home, but was wrapped in a blanket and carried home. A great welcome greeted me when I reached home, and I was placed in an improvised bed near a good fire. By now I was able to bear the light.

The first thing my many nurses did was to get my boots and stockings off and a new rig of clean clothes and a hot water bottle to my feet. The only drawback was that I could not see any preparations for a square meal. Although I was dying of hunger I was only allowed a spoonful of gruel every quarter of an hour.

I had several times asked to see my mother, and was told she was not well enough to see me, but would see me in two days. It was no wonder my dear mother was so ill, having gone through such mental agony of suspense, not expecting to see me alive.

As I write these lines, I feel thrilled with memories that shudder me, and you can imagine the unforgettable meeting of mother and son, who was lost, and, by the grace of God, was found.

Samuel concluded his account with a quotation from Psalm XL: 'I waited patiently for the Lord … and he heard my cry. He brought me also out of a horrible pit and out of the miry clay, and set my feet upon a rock.'

The editor of *The Herald* noted: 'Although Mr Lewis does not refer to it, we understand that Mr Lewis sends an annual contribution to Salem Chapel, Penycae, as a thanks offering for his escape. He has sent this annual subscription for sixty years.'

26

THE RED RIVER

When George Borrow began his walking tour of Wales in 1854, he arrived by train at Chester, and from there, wanting to start as he meant to go on, he walked to the house in Llangollen which he had booked as a base for himself, his wife and step-daughter, a distance of some twenty-five miles.

By the time he got as far as Ruabon, night had fallen, but he was undeterred. He wrote:

> I soon came to Rhiwabon – a large village about half way between Wrexham and Llangollen. I observed in this place nothing remarkable, but an ancient church. My way from hence lay nearly west. I ascended a hill, from the top of which I looked down into a smoky valley. I descended, passing by a great many collieries, in which I observed grimy men working amidst smoke and flame. At the bottom of the hill near a bridge I turned round. A ridge to the east particularly struck my attention; it was covered with dusky edifices, from which proceeded thundering sounds, and puffs of smoke. A woman passed me going towards Rhiwabon; I pointed to the ridge and asked its name; I spoke English. The woman shook her head and replied '*Dim Saesneg*' ('No English'). 'This is as it should be', said I to myself, 'I now feel I am in Wales.'

Borrow repeated his question in Welsh, for he was very proud of his ability to speak the language, and so learnt that what he could see was called Cefn Bach. Had he turned his back to the River Dee, and looked in the other direction, he would have had a view towards Gardden Woods and the Iron Age hill fort Y Gardden. It stands almost 600 feet above sea level, commanding fine views over the Marches across Wrexham County Borough and into England.

The name of this hill fort is derived from Caer-ddin, or fortified stronghold, and is similar to the Welsh name for Edinburgh, Caer-Edin. Y Gardden extends over about four acres, which are partly enclosed by a dry-stone wall and defended by two banks and three ditches. Though it has never been systematically excavated, it has been dated to about 400 BC and could have housed a community of considerable size. The local Iron Age people, the Deceangli (*Tegeingl* in Welsh), would have been its inhabitants until overcome by the Romans after 55 BC, though it is possible that it was still occupied even into the eighth century.

The little river Afon Goch flows down from Gardden Hill and joins Black Brook to continue eastward towards the Dee. Long after the Deceangli had left the hill fort, it was witness to a partly mythical, partly historical event, which has been remembered in a poem from the twelfth century explaining how the Afon Goch, or Red River, got its name.

There was once a bitter battle here, and the river ran red with the blood of the enemy. Owain Cyfeiliog, prince and poet, won the day, and the praise-poem to his warriors is considered by many scholars to be the work of Owain himself.

Owain was the nephew of Madog, Prince of Powys, and became Lord of Cyfeiliog, and ruler of most of southern Powys, on Madog's death in 1160. But before this, while still only under-lord to his uncle, he was already recognised as a poet of great originality, among the group known now as *Y Gogynfeirdd* (literally, 'the fairly early poets', to distinguish them from their predecessors, 'the early poets'). It seems as though Owain might have been an early example of that Chaucerian ideal of chivalry, '*a veray parfit gentil knight*'.

However, it should be acknowledged that he was also a pragmatist who changed sides more than once during his life, fighting at various times both for and against the English. Although we know that in 1188 Gerald of Wales was describing him as Henry II's close friend, in 1165 Owain was part of the Welsh alliance which drove Henry's army out of Wales.

In 1167 Owain took up arms once more. His brother Meurig had been captured by Gruffydd Maelor, their uncle Madog's son. Presumably Meurig was a pawn in the endless game of territorial acquisition which weakened the rulers of Wales throughout her history. He was held prisoner in the Maelor, an area now in Wrexham County Borough but then part of Powys Fadog, the northern section of the ancient kingdom of Powys, which had been divided only seven years previously on Madog's death.

When Owain came to war, however, it was not the Welsh war band of his cousin that he faced but Saxon and Norman mercenaries, there to take advantage of the lack of unity amongst the Welsh.

Their opposing forces met on the wooded slopes below the ancient hill fort of Y Gardden, and the battle's bloody aftermath gave the little Afon Goch its name.

Though Owain lost some good men, his warband carried the day and rescued Meurig, and a poem attributed to Owain himself celebrates those who fought beside him.

The poem is called *Hirlas Owain*, 'Owain's Horn', and its key image is the great blue drinking horn, the *corn hirlas*, which is passed around the feasting table to each warrior in turn. The poem, consciously modelled on the older Welsh battle poem *Y Gododdin*, paints a picture from the lives of a band of warriors and their leader.

A prince's drinking horn was usually made from a wild ox horn, which gave it the bluish colour to which the compound adjective *hirlas* ('long and blue') refers. Owain's was splendidly decorated with gold and silver. The horn was also known as *Corn Cychwyn*, 'the horn of beginning', and was the horn used to sound the charge or to signal that the warband was to set out.

In the poem, Owain's cupbearer carries the horn around the table and presents it to the warriors of the prince's victorious war band in turn. Each verse begins with a command to the cupbearer to pour. Then the poet tells us a little about the warriors and their prowess. Rhys, Gwgawn and Goronwy are all offered the horn. Cynfelen is already 'drunk with honour' and deserves the best mead; Gruffudd is called Owain's fearless dragon and apostrophised as 'a red spear to the enemy'.

In Morgant's hand the drinking horn is merry, and Gwestun the Great is praised for his untiring spirit on the battlefield. The poem recalls how their warband attacked the castle and set it on fire, and so released the gentle prisoner, Meurig, Gruffudd's son, a man whose power had been foretold. On his release, the long hills and the valley were bathed in sunshine.

The poet also remembers those who cannot drink, because they are numbered among the fallen. But the warriors will all meet again in paradise, where only truth is to be seen.

The poem is written in the complex pattern of chiming sounds called *cynghanedd*, or harmony, which is unique to Welsh poetry and, in my view, fiendishly difficult both to compose and to understand. This poem is an important example of early Welsh poetry.

Owain himself is a fascinating figure to follow through the twists and turns of twelfth-century warfare, diplomacy and strategy. Gerald of Wales recounts a story about Owain at table with the English king, Henry II, in Shrewsbury. Henry offered Owain bread with his own hand, which was considered a great honour and a mark of affection. Owain broke the loaf into pieces, as though it were communion bread, and solemnly laid the morsels out in a row, before picking them up one at a time to eat, until they were all gone. Henry's eyes never left this performance, and he asked Owain what he was doing.

'I am imitating you, my Lord,' replied Owain, with perfect equanimity, satirizing Henry's well-known habit of making as much as he could, piece by piece, from the church.

Owain seems, in later life, to have withdrawn from the world of statecraft and strategy. In 1170 he founded the Cistercian Abbey of Ystrad Marchell, near Welshpool. In 1195 he turned his kingdom over to his son Gwenwynwyn, after whom the southern Powys kingdom was subsequently named. Owain himself retired to his abbey at Ystrad Marchell, and two years later, at peace with himself and his god, he died there.

His poetry and the memories enshrined in the landscape and place names of Ruabon live on.

And a *Corn Hirlas*, carried with all ceremony by *Mam y Fro*, a 'mother of the area' (chosen by a panel of officials from the Gorsedd of the Bards for this solemn duty and honour, after written applications have been shortlisted) is offered to the Archdruid every year at the National Eisteddfod of Wales, as a symbol of welcome and hospitality.

27

ONE OF SIX

Each year since 1970, the Catholic Church in Wales remembers the Six Welsh Martyrs and their companions on their Feast Day, 25 October. Five of the six were Catholic priests put to death for their religious beliefs during the reigns of the Protestant Tudor and Stuart monarchs. The sixth was a Wrexham schoolteacher, whose courage and ready wit, even in terrible pain and fear, mark him out as a remarkable character.

His name was Richard Gwyn.

Richard was born in Llanidloes, at the beginning of the short reign of Henry VIII's son, Edward. It was a time when the common people were still reeling from the effects of Henry's annexation of Wales and his break with the Catholic Church. Richard's family, though not wealthy, was an old one, and they were practising Catholics.

Like many young Welsh scholars of his day, Richard went up to university in Oxford, but he only stayed there a short while, before moving to Cambridge to study under a Catholic, the Master of St John's College, George Bulloch. However, when the Protestant Elizabeth succeeded her Catholic half-sister Mary as queen, Richard's life was thrown into turmoil. His tutor, Dr Bulloch, was forced to resign, and soon fled abroad. Richard returned to Wales without being able to complete his studies.

He became a schoolmaster, moved to Wrexham and taught both in the town itself and in Overton, where he met and married his loyal wife Catherine. In time they had six children. Richard loved teaching. He wrote poetry. He seemed to be settled in a simple, fulfilling life. But he was being watched. He did not attend Anglican Communion. This was noted. Probably, like so many other Catholics during this period of religious persecution, he and Catherine went to secret Masses celebrated in someone's home.

He was denounced to the Bishop of Chester, who put great pressure on him to conform to the new religion … 'for his family's sake'.

After much heart-searching, and well aware of the fate that might face him and his family if he refused, Richard at last agreed, with a heavy heart. But an extraordinary thing happened, or so the chronicles relate.

As he left church after attending Anglican Communion for the first time, Richard was mobbed by a 'fearful company of crows and kites'. Tearing at him with beaks and claws, beating at him with their wings, creating an ear-splitting din, the birds pursued him home. He dragged open his front door and fell inside, calling for Catherine to help him bar the door, for he was weak and faint from fright. But being shut out did not stop the birds, which settled on the roof, beat against the door and – terror of terrors – scrabbled in the chimney, until Catherine built up the fire and made things too hot for them there.

As Catherine bathed Richard's scratched face, he stared at her with wild eyes.

'The Lord has sent these messengers to chastise me, for I have betrayed him,' he moaned. And he took to his bed.

Catherine feared for his life, for he was so pale, cold and still that she was sure he lay on his deathbed. But Richard, though outwardly motionless, was engaged in a fierce inner fight with his demons … and his conscience.

At last, in a thin voice, he called to Catherine. She hastened to his side, knelt, and took his hand in both her own. 'Tell me,' she whispered.

'I have offended the Lord. I must make amends. I must follow the true faith … whatever the cost. Do you understand me, Catherine dearest?'

'Yes, yes. I do. And I will support you Richard. I will not abandon you, whatever may befall us. We shall keep to the path: you, me, the children.'

He saw by the look in her eyes that she understood only too well what the cost might be. He saw, too, that she was not afraid. He sighed deeply, sat up and took her in his arms.

From that moment they were committed to a way of life that set them in constant conflict with the establishment and Elizabeth's harsh edicts, which aimed to crush any Catholic opposition to her rule.

Over the next few years, Richard, Catherine and their growing family moved house and school several times to avoid persecution. But at the same time he also became known as a poet, writing satirical verses, which, because they were popular, made the authorities ever more determined to silence him. In particular, Richard wrote poems satirising married priests. These, more than anything else, brought about his downfall.

The vicar of Wrexham was a priest who had conformed to the Anglican church and married. He was the butt of many of Richard's poems and he did not like it. He had Richard arrested and arraigned (that is, the charges against him were read out in his presence). As the clerk read, his vision blurred until he could no longer see. Helpless, he had to be led from the court and another clerk, trembling mightily, stepped up on the orders of the judge to take his place. Hushed whispers buzzed around the court and all eyes turned fearfully towards Richard. Was it a sign from God?

The judge spoke up suddenly: 'Let no man here speak of what he has seen, else the Papists will be making a miracle out if it.'

Reading the charges was completed without further incident, but from their faces, one might have thought that the steadfast Anglicans who filled the court were just as ready to believe in miracles as the Catholics against whom the judge's warning was directed.

Although the prisoner was arraigned, he did not stand trial. Somehow Richard escaped and went on the run. He managed to stay free for a further year and a half, constantly on the move from one safe house to another, seeing Catherine and the children secretly whenever and wherever he could, and keeping always just one step ahead of his pursuers.

But at last he could run no more: they caught up with him, and he was thrown into prison. For the next four years Richard was a captive: moved from one gaol to another, subjected to all kinds of punishments and pains.

But his spirit and his faith were strong, and his sense of humour, it seems, endured through all his troubles.

He was ordered to attend the Anglican service. When he refused, the sheriff sent six strong men to bring him from prison in his shackles and carry him bodily into church. They processed around the font and laid him down in front of the pulpit, for he was so trussed up that he could not stand. Richard, however, was determined not to hear any part of the service. He moved his legs so that the chains clashed and soon got up such a din that the priest could not be heard.

As a punishment, he was put in the stocks for a day, where a 'rabble of ministers' came to harangue him. But Richard was not to be cowed and gave as good as he got. One of the priests, whose nose was bulbous and red, taunted Richard, saying,

'I have just as much right to the keys of the church as Saint Peter!'

Richard's reply was tart and to the point: 'Peter received the keys of the Kingdom of Heaven, but the keys you were given obviously open the beer cellar!'

Richard was fined £280 for refusing to go to church and another £140 for the noise he made when he was taken there, defined by the court as 'brawling'. These were huge sums, and it must have been obvious that there was no way Richard could raise the money.

'What payment then, can you make towards the fines?' asked the judge, when Richard explained that he could not pay.

'Sixpence,' answered this mischievous and unquenchable spirit.

The judge was furious, and ordered a double set of manacles for Richard in retaliation. But Richard Gwyn was not a man who could easily be restrained from speaking his mind.

When eventually he was brought back to court with two fellow imprisoned Catholics, they were expecting to face the charges of the state. However, they found instead that a Puritan minister was waiting to preach to them. Determined not to listen, the resourceful trio began to harangue the preacher simultaneously in three different languages: Welsh, Latin and English. That soon put paid to the sermon!

Richard and his two companions, John Hughes and Robert Morris, were tortured and then tried for high treason in front of the Chief Justice of Chester. Witnesses accused the men of acknowledging the supremacy of the Pope and declaring that he was the equal of St Peter. In Richard's case there was an extra crime to be denounced, that he had recited 'certain rhymes of his own making' against married priests. The three men defended themselves with spirit and convincingly undermined the credibility of the witnesses. But in a judgment perhaps deliberately intended to divide and rule, the court found Richard and his friend John Hughes guilty but acquitted Robert Morris, apparently much to his chagrin.

When Richard and John Hughes were brought back to court for sentencing, John was reprieved and only Richard was condemned to death as a traitor to the crown. As the terrible brutalities of a traitor's death were read out in court, detailing how he was to be hung, then taken down, drawn and quartered, Richard, with astonishing tranquillity, only commented: 'What is all this? Is it any more than one death?'

The judge then turned his attention to Catherine, their new baby in her arms. She had been in court throughout the trial to support her husband. As the judge began to berate her and warn her not to follow in her husband's evil ways, Catherine spoke up: 'If it is blood you want, you may take my life as well as my husband's. Fetch the witnesses and give them a little bribe, and they will give evidence against me, too.'

She spent a few days in prison for this.

Richard went back to languish in gaol, and it is clear that he became close friends with his gaoler and the man's wife. Such close friends, in fact, that the gaoler had allowed Richard home on 'unofficial parole' to see his wife, which is why she had such a new baby. But when the authorities found out, they inflicted on the gaoler such a punishment that he wept in despair. He was ordered, on pain of imprisonment as a suspected Papist sympathiser if he refused, to be Richard's executioner. He had no choice but to carry out the dreadful deed.

When the fateful day came, Richard was led to the gallows in chains. Unwavering in his faith, he said the rosary on the knots in the rope holding up the chains. On the scaffold itself he was asked if he repented of his treason.

'I have never committed any treason more than your father or grandfather, unless it be treason to fast and to pray,' he said. Of course, the creed condemning him was so new that it had not even existed in the previous generation.

Richard then turned to the large crowd: 'I pray that you might all be reconciled with the true church,' he said, and followed this by asking for the forgiveness of anyone who had been offended by his poems or *carolau*, saying 'I have always been a jesting fellow.'

Then he calmly climbed the ladder and stood still as the noose was placed around his neck. When he was pushed off the ladder, he hung for some time, striking his chest with his hand in the gesture of a penitent asking for forgiveness. The executioner, hoping to put him beyond the misery of the rest of the suffering decreed by law, pulled on the heavy leg irons to try to finish him quickly. However, when his body was cut down for the second part of the threefold death, his disembowelment, Richard regained consciousness and remained aware of all that was happening as his body was cut open, dying only when his head was cut off. His last words, spoken in Welsh, were 'Jesus, have mercy on me.'

Though Richard was dead, his story was not quite finished. It seems that retribution reached out its long arms from beyond the grave to those who had condemned him. The judge became 'an idiot'; several members of the jury died prematurely and the court crier became 'a fool and a mumbler'.

Richard Gwyn was declared a saint in 1970. In one of the poems he wrote in gaol he described himself as 'A Welsh man, a teacher of children, who considers prison a small thing and still lives in hope.' He was prepared to die for his principles, yet still found the strength to joke and to hope. I admire, more than anything else, his spirited refusal to be silenced.

28

Balaclava Ned

Edwin Hughes, 'Balaclava Ned', was born in Wrexham on 12 December 1830 and baptised in St Giles' church early the following January. He died at the age of ninety-six in Blackpool, where he lived for the last seventeen years of his life, cared for by his daughter. In 1992 a plaque in his honour was unveiled on the house in Mount Street in Wrexham where he was born.

This Wrexham lad's claim to fame is that he was the longest-lived survivor of the Charge of the Light Brigade. Although he never came back to live in Wrexham once he had left, he was always a 'Wrexham boy' and his story merits being told.

Edwin was one of seven children. His parents, William and Mary, married in 1817. William was a tinsmith, and Edwin grew up in Mount Street at a time when Wrexham was expanding rapidly. He began making his living as a shoemaker, but at twenty-one years old he enlisted in the 13th Light Dragoons at Liverpool.

Dragoons were originally soldiers trained to fight on foot but travel on horseback for speed of movement. They were often used for scouting or reconnaissance work, and gradually their mounted role evolved so that they began to ride into battle. Because of their origin as scouts, they were more lightly armed than the 'heavy' regiments of horse. Their name comes from a firearm called the 'dragon' carried by the dragoons of the French Army and so seems very appropriate to a Welshman. Though many national armies, from Peru to Norway, have had dragoon regiments, the British Army was unique in downgrading all its cavalry regiments to dragoons during the eighteenth century as a money-saving device. They were trained in reconnaissance and skirmishing, and proved very successful regiments.

I don't know why Edwin Hughes decided to join
the Light Dragoons, nor what experience of horses
he had, though of course the long-established
pub The Nag's Head still stands in Mount
Street, not far from Edwin's childhood home.

He enlisted in November 1852 and
is recorded at that time as having sandy
hair, hazel eyes and a fresh complexion.
After two years of training he embarked
from Portsmouth for the Crimea with the 13th
Light Dragoons in May 1854. By September
he was fighting in the Battle of Alma, the
opening skirmish of the Crimean war.

The next action he saw was at the Battle of
Balaclava on 25 October 1854. This was when
the infamous Charge of the Light Brigade
took place.

Some say that it was because of a mis-
placed comma in the orders that the Light
Brigade, brandishing their swords, were
sent galloping down a narrow valley straight towards a Cossack
artillery battery containing twelve guns, with regiments of enemy
cavalry drawn up behind the guns.

Balaclava Ned

Others say that during the battle a messenger arrived with
written orders from the commander of the British force, Lord
Raglan. Lord Lucan, in charge of both the Light and the Heavy
Brigades, read the message. The orders read: 'Lord Raglan wishes
the cavalry to advance rapidly to the front, and try to prevent the
enemy from carrying away the guns.' Lord Lucan asked the messenger, Captain Nolan, which guns were meant; Nolan waved
his arm in a wide sweep, which must have encompassed both
the abandoned guns that Raglan actually meant and the Cossack
forces drawn up at the end of the North Valley. Lucan then ordered
the cavalry, led by Lord Cardigan, to advance. This they did at the
gallop, swords drawn, straight into the gun fire, down the valley
which the survivors came to call the Valley of Death.

Edwin Hughes was riding, by his own account, in the 'fifth file, front rank, right first of line'. His horse was shot from under him almost as soon as the 13th Light Dragoons came within range of the Russian guns, and he lay with his left leg trapped under its corpse for some time, though he said: 'I was damaged about the face and left leg but not seriously.' When the opportunity arose, he was helped to another horse and rode back. He was given the job of guarding Russian prisoners for the rest of the day.

Edwin was one of 122 men wounded. Out of the 600 who rode into the enemy guns over 50 were killed and 336 horses were killed or had to be destroyed. It took only twenty minutes to inflict this damage, and the action achieved no useful result. In fact, when Lord Lucan, charged to follow the Light Brigade at the head of the Heavy Brigade, saw what was happening, he ordered the Heavy Brigade to retreat, saying: 'They have sacrificed the Light Brigade: they shall not have the Heavy Brigade, if I can help it.' His decision meant that the survivors of the charge, who had broken through the enemy lines and were now behind their guns, found that they had no support. This emboldened the enemy to attack them again, and their return along the valley once again exposed them to heavy enemy fire.

The Charge of the Light Brigade has gone down in the annals of warfare as one of its most terrible blunders, and has been commemorated in film, literature and poetry, most notably by Tennyson but also by Kipling.

But what happened to 'Balaclava Ned' after that fateful event? By December he was in Scutari, where he was a cook at the General Depot, presumably until he was fit enough to rejoin his regiment, which he did the following May. Within two weeks, he was back in England.

He married in 1859, and he and his wife Hannah, also known as Annie, had four children. At least one of their children, according to the census of 1881, had been born in Canada, where he served two years with the regiment, matching the two years overseas service he had given in Turkey and the Crimea.

He remained with the Light Brigade for a total of twenty-one years, reaching the rank of troop sergeant major and receiving an allowance of one penny a day for 'good shooting', as well as a gratuity of £5, together with a medal for long service and good conduct. He also, of course, was awarded both the Crimean and the Turkish medals.

On his discharge from the Light Brigade in November 1873, at the age of forty-two, he was presented with a marble clock. He did not, however, remain a 'gentleman of leisure' for long. Before Christmas that same year he had become a sergeant instructor in the Worcestershire Yeomanry, rising to the rank of drill instructor and serving another twelve years before finally retiring from the army at the age of fifty-six.

He and Annie lived together in Birmingham until she died in 1899. After this, Edwin's eldest daughter, Mary, came to live with him and look after him. She seems to have cared for him for the rest of his life. The two of them moved in due course to Blackpool, where they lived peacefully.

'Balaclava Ned' died at the grand age of ninety-six, with his faithful daughter Mary at his side. He was buried on 23 May 1927 with full military honours in Blackpool Cemetery. As the coffin of this last, long-lived survivor of the Charge of the Light Brigade was lowered into the grave, trumpeters from his old regiment sounded The Last Post and Tennyson's poem 'The Charge of the Light Brigade' was read aloud. It seemed only fitting.

29

FRED AND FRANCES

Fred and Frances Plinston were traveling show people. Frances was born in a caravan, and fairs and shows were in her blood. Fred was born in 1874, the younger son of Samuel Plinston, a greengrocer from Warrington. Maybe it was marrying Frances that sparked his life-long love of the fair.

With his older brother Sam, Fred invented and built the first fairground ride known as The Cakewalk.

The Cakewalk was a style of dancing which originated in Florida around 1880 and was popular with African Americans. Sometimes plantation owners would bake a cake on Sundays and invite the neighbours over for a Cakewalk contest between their workers. In doing the Cakewalk, a couple promenaded in a dignified manner, high-stepping and kicking, mimicking high society. Whoever won would get the cake. The winner would cut the cake and share it with the others.

By the 1890s the Cakewalk was the hottest thing around and had moved from its country roots to become a big-city craze. The first formal Cakewalk contest was held in a New York ballroom in 1892.

The aim of Fred and Sam's Cakewalk fairground ride was to walk in the high-stepping Cakewalk style along gyrating troughs as they moved up and down, and to do this without falling over. The ride was powered by a steam engine set between the troughs.

In 1907 they opened their Cakewalk ride and toured it around Cheshire. They even took it to Hamburg Fair the same year, where Fred and Frances demonstrated the ride by dancing together on the machine.

There was strong anti-British feeling in Germany, although the First World War was still seven years away, so Fred and Sam called the ride 'The Brooklyn Cakewalk' and pretended it came direct from America. This seemed to do the trick, and the ride was very popular both in Germany and the UK.

At the great fair in London's Olympia, Fred, dressed in evening suit and white gloves, took the hand of the young Prince of Wales and led him over the Cakewalk. This prince, known to his family as David, ruled as king for less than a year before abdicating and becoming the exiled Duke of Windsor. As for Fred and Frances, it seemed as though things could not get better.

But some years later, Fortune's Wheel turned for them, and they were nearly ruined by a High Court case. They struggled for a while. At last they managed to bring together a small fair, much less grand than their Cakewalk, which toured Lancashire and Cheshire.

Eventually Fred and Frances, together with Fred's brother Sam and his wife Elsie, decided to settle in North Wales. They brought their little fair to Caergwrle in Flintshire, where they set up at the foot of the Castle Hill. Their children attended the infants' school there.

Times were hard and there was little money about. If a fair or other outdoor event were taking place nearby, Fred would make an effort to get a space there and take a coconut shy or some other game or ride. Their long-suffering horse Tommy pulled a cart loaded with all the equipment. A popular event was the sheepdog trial held at Rhydymwyn near Mold. This was about eight miles from their home, so Fred and Sam would set out early with the horse and cart, while Frances, Elsie and the children followed by train.

By 1918 Fred and Frances had rented a lock-up yard in Erddig Road for their caravan, and they felt themselves quite settled in Wrexham. They had mains water and toilet facilities, and were very proud of their 'home-on-wheels', which had top-quality woodwork and display cabinets for Frances' fine Dresden china. There was an electroplated wood-burning stove for both cooking and heating, and Fred built a portable kitchen, which he fitted up over the door to the caravan. Of course, it had to be taken down and packed away for traveling, and was very ingeniously designed to enable this to happen.

However, although their neighbours were full of friendly curiosity about the caravan, the Plinstons found themselves facing the same prejudice against travellers which is still all too frequent nowadays, and after two years the town council insisted that they give up their itinerant lifestyle and move into a house in Fairfield Street.

As is the case with many traveling people, it nearly broke Frances' heart to give up her 'palace on wheels' and move into a house, especially as the house was infested with cockroaches!

In the 1920s, Fred opened a new kind of stall with a gambling game called 'Electric Disc' and regularly took it to Wrexham Pleasure Fair, which opened the travelling people's season in early March each year.

One year, as the fair was being assembled on the Beast Market, Fred was helping the well-known showman Pat Collins to set up one of his rides, the 'Dragons'. It was a splendid machine and very ornate, with carved woodwork decorated with real gold leaf. The cars each had six rows of seats and were shaped at the front like dragons' heads, with open mouths and flared nostrils. These impressive vehicles, powered by electricity generated by a steam traction engine, dipped and reared as they revolved around a large organ, behind which a water cascade was picked out in coloured lights.

Whenever the 'Dragons' was being set up, the first thing to be positioned was always the organ, which travelled on a large four-wheeled truck with closed sides. The Beast Market, then in St George's Crescent, was on sloping ground, and the truck listed to one side as it was moved across. When one of the wheels hit a manhole cover, the vehicle, already unbalanced and dragged to a dangerous angle by its heavy load, started to keel over.

'Hang on to that side, boys!' yelled Pat Collins, so Fred and other men grabbed the side that had heaved up into the air. Their weight was enough to bring it down again, and disaster was averted.

Once it was made safe, Pat Collins took off his trademark bowler hat, mopped his brow and let fly some choice language about the careless handling of such a valuable load. If it had crashed, the damage would have been extensive, perhaps irreparable.

As well as its pipes, the organ boasted a percussion section of drums, cymbals and bells. There were also mechanical figures in uniform, one of which conducted, while the others 'played' famous popular and classical melodies and, of course, all the favourite tunes of the day.

Fred's son Albert was there with his father. He saw the near-disaster and wrote about it in later years in his memoir, concluding: 'I believe this organ still exists somewhere in England, owned by an enthusiastic collector. It would be worth many thousands of pounds now ... as long as it has remained unharmed!'

30

TWO SAINTS

Wrexham's fine parish church, which archaeologists believe to be the third built on the site, dates from the end of the fifteenth century. It stands on Bryn-y-Grog, which means the Hill of the Cross, but, like many churches, it has its own legend of divine intervention in the choice of site.

Work on the building was begun, in the unspecified 'once upon a time' of such stories, on Brynffynnon, the Hill of the Well. It seemed a good place. But whatever was achieved each day was undone each night. The workers would arrive bright and early, only to find their neatly stored tools tumbled, the stacked stones scattered and the freshly dug foundation ditches full of rubble. Whatever was interfering with their work, it was silent and implacable. They grew increasingly uneasy as time went by and the destruction continued.

At last, the unnerved men decided to keep watch, to find out who ... or what ... was causing the problem. Since no one was brave enough to stay there alone, they decided they would all stay, on the grounds that there would be safety in numbers, no matter what they had to face.

And so it was, that, in the very darkest part of the night, they were all there to see the day's work collapse at an unseen hand and to hear a disembodied and resounding voice cry out: 'Bryn-y-Grog! Bryn-y-Grog!'

They took this as a divine sign, and the work was moved forthwith the few hundred yards that were all that separated the Hill of the Well and the Hill of the Cross. From that time, all their problems disappeared, and the work proceeded apace.

The church is dedicated as the parish church of St Giles, and this name dates back to at least 1494. Its 'steeple' is counted as one of the Seven Wonders of Wales in the old rhyme, though it is, in truth, a tower rather than a steeple. Maybe there was a steeple before the great wind of 25 November 1330 blew down the elevated portions of the church, but after that it was definitely rebuilt as a tower, for that is what stands today. At the time, the destruction was regarded as just retribution for holding the market on a Sunday, and so market day was changed to Thursday. It is now held on a Monday.

The church contains images of St Giles in wood, in stone and in glass, but many believe that the church was originally dedicated to the Celtic saint Silyn.

Both names can be rendered in Latin as *Aegidius*, and this may be the source of the confusion. However, there may also be an indication that the origins of the church date back to the times of Celtic Christianity, for the Celtic pantheon saints were not necessarily recognised by the Roman Catholic Church. When the Marches came under Norman influence, many church communities tactically changed allegiance to a more acceptable patron.

Giles and Silyn both have their legends, which are very different.

Silyn, also sometimes spelt Sulien, is the one about whom less is known. He was the brother of Saints Rhystud, Gadarn, Dwywau, Derfel and Cristiolus. His full name was Silyn ap Hywel ab Emyr Llydaw. *Ap* and *ab* are forms of the patronymic 'son of', and Llydaw is the Welsh name for Brittany, where Silyn was also venerated.

He trained at Llancarfan and the great seat of ecclesiastical learning, Llanilltud Fawr, also called Llantwit Major, on the south coast of Wales. He founded at least two religious communities in the north east of the country: one at Llansilin and another near Wrexham, called Capel Silin.

He eventually settled, with his companion Cadfan, on the holy island of Bardsey, off the extreme northwest tip of Wales. Bardsey has been a place of pilgrimage for centuries. In fact, three visits to Bardsey were reputed to equal one pilgrimage to Rome in their efficacy. It was known as the burial place of 10,000 saints, using the word in the Celtic way, to mean holy man, rather than miracle worker.

Giles' legend, which dates from the tenth century, is more detailed.

He was born an Athenian, and travelled to Nîmes, near the mouth of the River Rhône, where he became a hermit and settled in a remote cave. There he was befriended by a hind, which nourished him on its milk and so kept him alive.

One day the king of the Visigoths, by name Wamba, was out hunting and gave chase to the hind. It fled into a thicket, and Wamba shot an arrow after it. When he broke though the undergrowth in pursuit, he found Giles with his arms around the hind and Wamba's arrow in his shoulder. Wamba was impressed by Giles' fortitude and holiness, for he refused any treatment for the wound, saying 'My strength is made perfect in weakness.' For this reason, Giles is the patron saint of those who are wounded or crippled, and among the many churches dedicated to him is St Giles Cripplegate in London.

Wamba decided to dedicate the land where he had met Giles to God, and built a monastery there, at Saint Gilles in Provence. Giles was its first abbot.

Giles' reputation for sanctity became so great that the Emperor Charlemagne came to the monastery to confess his sins to Giles. Among his sins was one so terrible that Charlemagne dared not name it. As Giles celebrated Mass the next day, an angel appeared, carrying a chart. Upon it was written, in letters of flame, the nature of Charlemagne's sin. Giles prayed over it, and as he did so, the letters disappeared. The legend does not make it clear whether Giles read them before they were gone!

Giles lived a long time as abbot and attracted many followers to the monastery by his holiness, but as he grew old he began to long once more for the solitude and peace of his former life as a hermit. So he made a pilgrimage to Rome, where he offered the monastery to the Pope.

The Pope, however, commanded him to carry on with his ministry and gave Giles a gift for the monastery: two doors of fine cypress wood. Giles, perhaps piqued by the Pope's refusal to relieve him of his burden and grant his request, threw the doors into the sea.

However, the wind and the waves miraculously carried the doors across the Mediterranean to the southern coast of France, until they drifted ashore. Giles found them, still in perfect condition, floating in the swamps of the Camargue, barely ten miles from his monastery at Nîmes. He took this as a sign that he, like his doors, was meant to be there.

Giles remained at the monastery until his death, when his relics, which were venerated throughout the Middle Ages, were set in a jewelled shrine in Toulouse, on the pilgrims' paths to both Santiago de Compostela in southern Spain and the Holy Land.

As well as being the patron saint of cripples and lepers, because of his unhealed wound, he is also the patron saint of nursing mothers, in honour of the hind which suckled him. For some reason, he is also the patron saint of blacksmiths, and his shrines were often found at crossroads and junctions, to allow riders to pray to him while their horses were being shod.

There are more than 160 churches dedicated to St Giles in Britain. His healing powers are considered so effective that over twenty hospitals also bear his name. In Germany he is known as one of the Fourteen Holy Helpers, saints who can intercede directly on behalf of sinners with God. Wrexham has a powerful patron saint!

NOTES

INTRODUCTION

For more on the history of Wrexham see www.cpat.org.uk/ycom/wrexham/wrexham.pdf and *Real Wrexham* by Grahame Davies.

If you would like to read Mabon's story and the rest of Culhwch and Olwen, since I couldn't include it in this collection, I recommend Sioned Davies' translation of *The Mabinogion* (Oxford University Press, 2007).

1: THE MASSACRE OF THE MONKS

The story of Augustine's role in foretelling and ensuring the massacre of the monks of Bangor-on-Dee comes largely from Theophilus Evans' *Drych y Prif Oesoedd*, literally translated as 'a mirror of the early times'. This book, published in Bangor in 1740, is described in the National Library of Wales' *Dictionary of Welsh Biography* as a 'prejudiced and uncritical but very entertaining version of the early history of Wales'. Bede, writing in AD 731, gave an alternative version, more favourable to Augustine, in his *Ecclesiastical History of the English People* (book 2, chapter 2). Geoffrey of Monmouth gave a third account of the same events in his *History of the Kings of Britain* (xi 12 and 13).

2: JACK MARY ANN

With thanks to my friend David Mawdsley, a volunteer signalman on the Llangollen Railway, for detailed advice on the technicalities of early twentieth-century railway procedures. He wrote, in part:

It is clear from the Disused Stations website that the Moss Valley branch was single track, but probably with loops at intervals to allow trains to pass each other. The fundamental principle of a single-track railway is that only one train is allowed into the section between passing loops at any one time. This is achieved by having a token (and only one) for each section, without which the driver of a train is not allowed to proceed. But even with this precaution it can go wrong – see, for example, the accounts of the head-on collision at Abermule near Newtown in *c*.1921.

It could be that one or other driver had passed a signal at danger and proceeded without being in possession of the token. A more likely explanation, however, is that the brakes on the loaded coal train had failed, with the result that the train was, in railway terminology, 'running away'. Given that the coal train would be very heavy and heading downhill, that possibility is not at all unlikely.

When anything untoward occurs, the signalman's first reaction is to put all signals to danger immediately. In your story, that would not stop the coal train 'running away', as it must already have passed a signal at danger. There would be a chance, however, that the passenger train could be stopped a safe distance away, giving the driver of the coal train a chance to bring his train under control.

Having put all signals to danger, the signalman's next option is to divert one or other of the trains, so as to prevent the head-on collision. Whether that would have been possible in the circumstances of your story would depend upon the specific layout of the Moss branch, which of course disappeared many years ago. But it is possible that there would have been a loop or siding into which the signalman could divert one or other of the trains.

I shudder to think what the consequences of this scenario might have been. Unless the driver of the passenger train was particularly alert, he would think the signalman was mistaken in trying to turn his train into a loop or siding. But if the coal train was diverted into a loop or siding, the chances are that it would derail when passing over the points at speed. Even if it stayed on the track, it would probably have hit the buffers at the end of the siding and promptly derailed. In either case, the derailment would almost certainly have blocked the main line, so giving rise to a risk that the passenger train would strike or be struck by the debris!

4: ALICE IN THE CIRCLE: ST MARY'S SCHOOL GHOST

With thanks to: Caitlin, Charlotte, Chloe, Cody, Ellie, Holly, Ioan, Jack, Kyle, Lauren, Tegan and everyone in Mrs Prescott's class at St Mary's Aided Primary School, Brymbo; Mr Parry, the school caretaker; Mrs Roberts, who arranged for me to meet Year 6; and Mr Jones, the headteacher.

5: FAUNA AND FLORA

From *Maes Maelor* by R.J. Jones (Swansea, Gwasg John Penry, 1957) – my translation from the original Welsh – kindly lent by Les Barker, and *Reflections of a Bygone Age* by R. Lowe (Wrexham, Bridge Books, 1998), kindly lent by Peter Jones.

Field Marshall Frederick Roberts, created Earl Roberts in 1900 for his service during the Boer War, was born in India: his Irish father was a general and his Scottish mother a major's daughter. A career serviceman, he was awarded many honours, including the Victoria Cross in India in 1858. His son, also Frederick Roberts, and also holder of the Victoria Cross, was killed during the Boer War.

6: THE KING OF THE GIANTS

I am grateful to Dez and Ali Quarrell of Mythstories Museum in Wem, Shropshire, who told me this tale, which they collected from people living in the area of Whixall Moss. This is the bog in which the knights were lost. Their informants did not give information about an exact location for the giant king's court, so I have identified two possible sites with ancient connections to the *tylwyth teg*, one in and one near the town of Wrexham.

Caer Alyn is the site of a community archaeological and heritage project, with a website at www.caeralyn.org. The Fairy Mound is in a private garden, and not accessible to the public. A hollow oak, which still stands on its summit, was popularly supposed to be where the *tylwyth teg* danced, and in the 1860s, while the barrow was still in an open field, local children would gather there at dusk, hoping to see them.

7: WARTIME TALES

With thanks to: Mary Hughes, Betty Jones, Kris Morrison, Audrey Owens, Diane Parry, Margaret Roberts, Kathleen Smith, Betty Thompson and Dennis Williams, whose stories were published in *Memories of Pontcysyllte* by Amy Douglas and Fiona Collins, eds (Tempus, 2006). *Nain* is the North Wales word for grandmother, and *taid* for grandfather.

8: THE RED HAND OF CHIRK

Jane Barlow of Brymbo Heritage Group told me that the 'red hand' actually denotes a bought title. In *Dr Johnson and Mrs Thrale's Tour in North Wales, 1774*, introduction and notes by Adrian Bristow (Wrexham, Bridge Books, 1995), p 120, Mrs Thrale wrote in her diary entry for 7/9/1774:

> Chirk Castle is by far the most enviable dwelling I have yet ever seen, ancient and spacious, full of splendour and dignity, yet with every possible convenience for obscurity and retirement. Here we saw the best Library we have been shewn [*sic*] in Wales, and a ridiculous Chaplain whose conversation with Mr Johnson made me ready to burst with laughing.

9: IN THE BLACK PARK

This version is retold from *The Pedestrian's Guide through North Wales* by George John Bennett (London, 1838). Bennett writes that Mary and Owen's initials could still be seen carved into the stump that was all that remained of a great elm tree. Also from Richard Holland, *Supernatural Clwyd* (Gwasg Carreg Gwalch, 1989).

10: Mining Tales

Information about mining superstitions and the humorous tales comes from an article 'Aspects of Mining Folklore in Wales' by Lynn Davies, published by St Fagan's National History Museum. The story of John Evans' survival comes from *Real Wrexham* by Grahame Davies (Seren, 2007). Information about the Gresford disaster and the text of the ballad of the same name are widely available online.

11: The Three-Way Crossroad

Philip Yorke's account comes from *A History of the Parish of Marchwiel*, Cynthia Rees (Bridge Books, 1998).

12: The River that Runs in the Sky

With thanks to Patricia Diggory and Karen Wright for sharing their family memories, first published in *Memories of Pontcysyllte*, Amy Douglas and Fiona Collins, eds. (Tempus, 2006). The story about George Borrow comes from his *Wild Wales* (Bridge Books, 2002 ed.).

13: A Living Witness

For more on the period of the Battle of Crogen, see story 26, The Red River.

14: A Wrexham Werewolf

Amy Douglas told me about this story, which she found on: www.davidicke.com/forum/showthread.php?t=16126. You can also read it on www.werewolfpage.com/myths/wales.htm.

15: The Marriage of Owain Glyndŵr

For a fuller survey of Glyndŵr's career and its political implications, see chapter 5 of John Davies' *A History of Wales* (Penguin, 1994).

16: The Boys Beneath the Bridge

From Gordon Emery's *Curious Clwyd II* (Masons Design and Print, 1996), kindly lent by Les Barker, and generally widely collected.

17: Robin Ruin's Ruin

I found the bones of this gruesome tale in the A.N. Palmer Centre, Wrexham Museum, in a booklet called 'Overton in Times Past – a Brief History', by Brian Done and Betty Williams (Shire Hall, Mold, 1992).

18: The Old Un o' the Moor

From R.J. Jones' *Maes Maelor* (Swansea, Gwasg John Penry, 1957). This is my translation from the original Welsh. (It was kindly lent by Les Barker.)

19: Lady Blackbird

The gothic 'cottage orné'-style buildings with the crosses post date the story, for Margaret died in 1713 and the cottages were nearly all built between 1805 and 1816 by George Boscawen, who inherited the estate through his wife after the male line of the Trevors died out in 1743.

20: Dancing with the Fair Folk

Information about the fairies' dance and how to rescue someone from them using mountain ash comes from John Rhys' *Celtic Folklore* (Oxford University Press, 1901).

21: Offa's Offspring

Asser's Life of Alfred can be read online in a translation from 1906 at archive.org/details/asserslifeofking00asseiala.

22: SOME WONDERS OF OVERTON

There is basic information about Grand National winners at www.aintree.co.uk/index.php?content=pages&id=grand-national-winners&p=4. I found out about Poethlyn from Brian Done and Betty Williams' *Overton in Times Past: A Brief History* (Shire Hall, Mold, 1992). The image of the vintage cigarette card comes from my own collection.

23: THE WITCH OF PENLEY

'Witchcraft in Seventeenth-Century Flintshire (Part Two)' by J. Gwynn Williams, M.A. (*Journal of the Flintshire Historical Society*, 1975–1976, 27, p. 5–35), www.llgc.org.uk/index.php?id=575.

24: THE PIG OF THE VALLEY: JOHN ROBERTS THE CUNNING MAN

I found this story in both Richard Holland's *Supernatural Clwyd* (Gwasg Carreg Gwalch, 1989) and W. Jenkyn Thomas' *The Welsh Fairy Book* (Dover, 2001 ed.) in which it is told about Robin Ddu, but is so similar to this well-known story about Mochyn y Nant that I have borrowed details from both.

25: BURIED ALIVE FOR EIGHT DAYS

From *The Rhos Herald*, April and May 1932.

26: THE RED RIVER

Pol Wong told me about the legend and I found more in Aled Lewis Evans' book *Bro Maelor* (Gwasg Carreg Gwalch, 1996). The quotation from George Borrow comes from his *Wild Wales* (Bridge Books, 2002 ed.). The story from Gerald of Wales is in *The Journey Through Wales* (Penguin, 1978 ed.).

The text of *Hirlas Owain* can be found at www.wrexham.gov.uk/english/heritage/medieval_exhibition/long_blue_original_welsh.htm.

An English rendering in rhyming verse by Robert Williams, which is not very close to the original Welsh, can be read at: www. bartleby.com/270/1/582.html. For more on the Battle of Crogen in which Owain also fought, see story 13: A Living Witness.

27: One of Six

The bones of this information come from two sources: the website of St Richard Gwyn School, Flint, and www.angelusonline.org. The extract from the poem reads as follows in the original (it is my translation):

> Athro plant o Gymro
> Sydd yn kymryt karchar beth
> Yn byw mewn gobeth eto.

28: Balaclava Ned

You can find absolutely everything you want to know about the soldiers who took part in the Charge of the Light Brigade at this website (this is the page for Balaclava Ned), www.chargeofthelightbrigade.com/allmen/allmenH/allmenH_13LD/hughes_e_1506_13LD.html.

29: Fred and Frances

Much of the information about the Plinstons in this chapter comes from the memoirs of their son Albert, held by Wrexham Library. According to the web site www.traditionalrides.com, the Plinston's Cakewalk is still in use, and can be seen at such events as Nottingham Goose Fair and Llandudno Vintage Weekend.

30: Two Saints

Information about Silyn and Giles comes mainly from *The Book of Welsh Saints* by T.D. Breverton (Glyndŵr Publishing, 2000) and *The Oxford Dictionary of Saints* by David Farmer (Oxford University Press, 2004 ed.).

BIBLIOGRAPHY

Bagshaw, J., *Broughton Then and Now* (Bridge Books, 1992)

Bede, *The Ecclesiastical History of the English People*, Book II (Oxford University Press, 1994 ed.)

Bennett, G.J., *The Pedestrian's Guide through North Wales* (London: H. Colbourn, 1838)

Borrow, G., *Wild Wales* (Bridge Books, 2002 ed.)

Breverton, T.D., *The Book of Welsh Saints* (Glyndŵr Publishing, 2000)

Bristow, A. (Intro), *Dr Johnson and Mrs Thrale's Tour in North Wales 1774* (Bridge Books, 1995)

Brut y Tywysogion

Davies, G., *Real Wrexham* (Seren, 2007)

Davies, J., *A History of Wales* (Penguin, 1994)

Dutton, R.J.A., *Hidden Highways of North Wales* (Gordon Emery, 1997)

Dodd, A.H. (ed), *A History of Wrexham* (Bridge Books, 1957)

Done, B. and William, B., *Overton in Times Past: A Brief History* (Shire Hall, Mold, 1992)

Douglas, A. and Collins, F. (eds), *Memories of Pontcysyllte* (Tempus, 2006)

Emery, G., *Curious Clwyd II* (Masons Design and Print, 1996)

Evans, A.L., *Bro Maelor* (Gwasg Carreg Gwalch, 1996)

Evans, T., *Drych y Prif Oesoedd* (Bangor, 1740)

Farmer, D., *The Oxford Dictionary of Saints* (Oxford University Press, 2004 ed.)

Geoffrey of Monmouth, *The History of the Kings of Britain* (Penguin, 1966 ed.)

Gerald of Wales, *The Journey through Wales* (Penguin, 1978 ed.)

Holland, R., *Supernatural Clwyd* (Gwasg Carreg Gwalch, 1989)

Jones, R.J., *Maes Maelor* (Gwasg John Penry, 1957)

Lowe, R., *Reflections of a Bygone Age* (Bridge Books, 1998)

Parry, T. (ed.), *The Oxford Book of Welsh Verse* (Oxford University Press, 1962)

Rees, C., *A History of the Parish of Marchwiel* (Wrexham, 1998)

Rhys, J., *Celtic Folklore: Welsh and Manx* (Oxford University Press, 1901)

Thomas, W.J., *The Welsh Fairy Book* (Dover, 2001 ed.)

Vesey, G., *Philip Yorke: Last Squire of Erddig* (Bridge Books, 2005)

Williams, D., *Dating the Past in North-Eastern Wales* (Gwasg Carreg Gwalch, 2004)

Williams, W.A., *The Encyclopaedia of Wrexham* (Bridge Books, 2010 ed.)

ARTICLES

Davies, L., 'Aspects of Mining Folklore in Wales', *Folk Life*, vol. 9 (St Fagan's National History Museum, December 1971)

Done, B. and William, B., 'Overton in Times Past – A Brief History' (Shire Hall, Mold, 1992)

Williams, J.G., 'Witchcraft in Seventeenth-Century Flintshire' (*Journal of the Flintshire Historical Society*, 1975–1976, 27, p. 5–35)